Welcome
to
Gomorrah

WELCOME
to
GOMORRAH

Niall Quinn

WOLFHOUND PRESS

First published 1995 by
WOLFHOUND PRESS Ltd
68 Mountjoy Square
Dublin 1

and Wolfhound Press (UK)
18 Coleswood Rd
Harpenden
Herts AL5 1EQ

Wolfhound Press receives financial assistance from the Arts Council/An
Chomhairle Ealaíon, Dublin.

British Library Cataloguing in Publication Data
A catalogue record for this book is available from the British Library.

The author acknowledges the assistance of an Arts Council Bursary
while working on this book.

ISBN 0 86327 460 9

Typesetting: Wolfhound Press
Cover design: Daire Ní Bhréartúin
Cover painting: 'St Lucia — Forest Parrot Chatter' 1992 by Tony O'Malley by
kind permission of the artist
Text motif is based on a pre-hispanic stamp design, redrawn by Jorge Enciso and
published in his book *Designs from Pre-Columbian Mexico* (Mexico, 1947)
Printed in Ireland by Betaprint, Dublin

It has been a long, harsh journey, from here to there, and, Lia, I've had to retrace each step.

Life is quite handsome to me now, and the days are as wholesome as fresh bread. I like this quality, this firm, well-tailored quality in the autumn, the fall, of my years.

Ivory white shirts, broadcloth suits, easy-fitting brogues. An ample breakfast in solitude, and dinner in a candlelit atmosphere. Early to bed, by nine at the latest, and some well-bound Old Master in vellum. A good mattress, sweet sheets, a solid read and a sound sleep. I am happy now. An elder statesman in the domain and empire of myself, and not subject to the tentative probings of foreign forces upon my peace and serenity. Secure boundaries in isolated lands in my mind. I watched the sunset tonight, Lia. It was all in colour. In millions of nameless colours. All were warm and glowing and happy as one by one they disappeared into infinity. I feel benevolence towards all that is past. And to all my dead years whose ashes are already scattered to the winds, I raise a glass, a long-chilled glass full of ice and lemon, and gold rum and tonic. And to you, Lia: Always. I never saw her preen. Nor was there ever any touch of maquillage in her manner or attitude. These defects I have always found in women, young women, and all men, especially myself.

I saw a cat like that, on a bad winter's day on a mountainside. A half-wild cat, abandoned when it was a kitten, and who had somehow survived. Traces of domesticity lingered about its manner, but only just. When I gave it one of my precious sardines, it squatted down and ate the fish, contentedly. And I ate all of the rest in peace. There was a look of gentle, bashful fear about the cat's eyes as it rose and left.

I often saw that cat on the mountain, but it never approached me again. I was spiritual at that time and felt it wanted me to know it had come in a desperate hunger to me, and had lost its pride in the journey. And that it was my fault; and would be my responsibility, always.

The first moment I ever saw Lia I remembered that cat. But pride can be regained, and the cat knew that. There are feats awaiting, and even the feat of drawing oneself up to try again from the desolation of defeat removes the sting of shame and the taste of humble-pie. It can dim, even quench, the memory. Our past is as easily forgotten as all of our lives. There is a continuity from here to there, yes, but there is always a bend in the river. I knew that, then.

She was just another prostitute standing at the other side of the dock gates. And I was something less than just another illegal European migrant to Brazil. I was broken in mind and spirit, and started every day with a tablet of some description or a glass of whiskey. And my finances at that time, having placed a ten dollar note in my passport when I presented it to the immigration official, amounted to sixty-seven US dollars. Enough, perhaps, to have her as a whore five or six times. Hence are young women the markers of the coin of every realm. Thus I had enough to live for a month in this country, living in poverty, and then creation would fall upon me. And she was just another woman, no, she was, then, still just a girl and reaching through to my consciousness like an emerging dream.

I felt her kinship. I had never seen her before, but she was not a stranger. Our eyes were already anticipating each other with eagerness, with prodigal joy.

But she was just another girl earning her food and shelter in just another awful manner.

She knew; it showed in her smile. But she was smiling, anyway. Smiling gallantly. It was very nourishing to me to see that gallantry.

I saw that smile once again, the day she had the row with Papa; the first day that she met our adopted Papa.

She was the first to warn me, right after I'd pushed through the turnstile, although I already knew, that it wasn't safe for me to walk along these streets, not even in the broad, mid-morning sunshine.

There were armed soldiers everywhere on these dockside roads. And armed thugs were forever moving deftly, swiftly, and killingly through the swarm, as naturally as hunting animals felling prey always near a water-hole. And here, with ships and cargoes and sailors and tourists, was a rich, lush watering hole where the fattest of prey just loitered and strolled about. Wounded prey, prey carrying any wound in mind or body, were instinctively detected, and hunted first.

All this was easily soothed by my chemical tranquillity, and could not in the least surprise me. What astonished my haze of sedation was that she spoke in German.

'Are you a German, perhaps?' were my first words to her, and when she answered I saw a look of disappointed exasperation mask her face. She was no more German, despite all her Aryan features tanned and glowing with warm Brazilian blood, than I.

'I can't myself remember that,' she said.

There were two men shouting at us now, in anger, dangerous anger and rage that was almost instantly murderous. She was unperturbed, but I anyway stepped in front of her.

'Oh!' she said, and I could hear the smile, 'Oh I like that!' And then we had to ignore the taunts, the threats, the obscene gestures of the outraged taximen cheated of their rip-off, with the street-children joining in for any fun, or any evil, until we reached the bus no more than twenty-five metres away. Once aboard we were no more vulnerable than anyone else. But still most primely vulnerable.

The danger was palpable. At any second, anywhere, a gun or a knife will attack the primacy of your life, and hurriedly, but with the casual skill of a slaughterer, lay you waste.

The urgency of the need for money was on so many faces. It was a rubbed-raw, sexual, impatient greed. It was a silently screeching addicted lust, scowling and full of hate, to get a piece of whatever was going, and fuck the consequences. The entire culture of an entire stratum of society was to get a buck, hook or crook. It was a consuming, implacable and ancient obsession. Hang loose, hunt prey, and get a goddamn buck. The relentless lust of its appetite could never be sated. Each feed merely reinforced it. Nowhere else but on the streets, minute after minute, hour after hour, day and night, could it find and sup temporary remission. Lia gave me a smile from her repertoire of smiles. It had that touch of fear and bashfulness, like the mountain cat's.

She was all of smiles, of hues of smiles, all the tropical colours of happiness.

I began to tell her of a mountain cat I had once known, that spoke to me in English, Irish and Latin. A trilingual cat. Her face snapped into open bewilderment, and then she listened. And with disbelieving eyes she believed all. When I finished she immediately began to repeat the story to herself in Portuguese, stopping occasionally to ask for additional information. Yes, the cat had a name, a full name: Kerry Ireland. No, he wasn't bedraggled; he always, even in the mountains, wore immaculately white gloves and an immaculately white shirt, and his furcoat was always freshly cleaned and brushed. She shook with laughter.

Thus the half-hour bus journey to Itaqui was whiled away. And she had not asked me one question about myself; where I was from or why I had come.

I was already in love with her; now I began to admire and like her, too.

My experiences of women, under all rubrics, have been horrific. I consider them capable of the greatest foulness, deceit, and evil. Smug, conceited, and rock-firm in their unquestioned convictions and their avaricious conceits. But above all it is their cruelty, their remorseless cruelty, and their selfishness, their sneaking, smiling, loathsome selfishness that revolts me. Their essence is power. They cringe to it and adore it, and use it without mercy. Their contempt for weak or diffident men, as distinct from their self-indulgent care of broken men, is absolute. They are never weak nor timid with power. At any age it is massively aphrodisiacal to them and enraptures them to a hellish place far beyond common sadism. To the serious triteness of the business and political world they bring with them the further triteness of little girls most competently playing trite housewife, and copy most faithfully all of the shabby incompetence of that.

Motherhood is neither their forte nor their *raison d'être*. They have turned its glory into a martyrdom to be worn and displayed as a halo. Children are their unquestionable meal-tickets and their excuse for making nothing of their lives. And with cosmic justice, from the cradles they rock — and so often rear with so much cruelty — come the men they most hate, despise and fear: rapists. Perhaps that is why females exercise no understanding of the vulnerability, the fragility, and the marvel, of the ceaselessness of human endeavour and the human need to transcend the petty squabbles of life. The pettiness of life is all to them. The purdah or liberation of their normality, their gifts, their talents, is neither imposed nor granted. And they know that. They know that's true.

It is what they want, connive, demand and get to suit themselves in particular circumstances at particular times. It lies within them, and when unused to their satisfaction the guilt is placed on man; he is made, by them, to bear and feel it as his lawful burden and cross. Women are not of the nature of children, they are of the nature of limp velleities. I do not like women. I am heterosexual and I do not like women. I wish I could say they were good for sex, if nothing else. But that myth, nubilely maintained by their younger sisters in the transient heat of their transient mating bloom, is a guffaw of spite in the face of actuality, of reality. They do enjoy the well-cultivated mirage of their sexual powers over men, but their enjoyment of sex must be coaxed and forced and fretted from them. A man's human need for sexual fulfilment is a frivolous joke to them. They will sheath him in plastic and thus render themselves virtual plastic dummies to him and expect him to be satisfied. They are never so stupid as to entertain any liking nor care for men, other than as paycheque providers.

This is not eccentric garbage, though it is garbage nevertheless, and I realised that. But it lies, like common racism, like parochialism, just under the skin, and any sharp inconvenience, any shadow of threat, the most minor of hurts, will bring it gushing out. All this is overtly pale, gentle and mild when contrasted with the daily banter of the officers' messroom on the Dutch ship that brought me to Brazil. The participants in that thrice daily ordeal looked forward not to the innate joy and musical warmth of the Brazilian people so at odds with their own dour and dourly regimented society and manners and thoughts. They looked forward to whores. And they would ram it into the little bitches until it really hurt, really give it to them hard, make the fucking bitch scream for it, make her beg, and then really slap it to her. Again, and again, and again.

This is, in a normal relationship, a source of legitimate and excellent pleasure, and it is, thus, one more marker of the despair of the human condition.

Nevertheless, all of my experiences with women have been horrific. And I would not wish to repeat any. I would do amazing things to avoid a repetition of any.

Thus, alongside the bus now parked in a side square of downtown Itaqui, I slipped five dollars into her palm as I shook hands with her: goodbye. She looked appalled. By the money or the gesture or the announcement. I never knew. There was a bedlam of emotions flashing in her eyes, but most of all she looked appalled. Her head bowed for an instant. Then she said she needed time. She said it in an indifferent manner and I believed her. But the limit of my compromise was to agree to share a beer with her. Hostile reality was stalking me now and I had no more stories to tell. I needed to be alone. Because I was helpless to the approaching reality of my condition I needed to be alone. I had just entered the forty-fourth year of my life and I hoped, day by day, that tomorrow wouldn't come. My mind had been wounded. Nothing staunched the flow of that pain, no hands reached to staunch the flow of that mental blood. I was holding mental hands over the wound, and was blinded by pain and horror. I took tablets to keep me sedated, but they really only eased the breathing. They did nothing for the pain. Alcohol made me forget it, and I needed to die with the pain, if not forgotten, at least not present. I needed, deeply, to be alone; to die or to recuperate. If sympathy is a learned, a cultured, response, I suppose I was, unwillingly and in the heat of argument, asking for her sympathy. But I had become cultured to greet sympathy with reserve. I could not properly accept it.

And during the row that dragged these words from me she addressed me by a name that was never mine, but which she continued, thereafter, to use as my given name. I had waited all my life to be just so named, and thereafter adopted it as my own.

She said she was sharing Sylvia's room. Sylvia was a smug, professional prostitute and with great certainty predicted Lia's direful end, but only in the manner of speaking about what might have been. But she needed a place to stay during the nights, and it was the most impossible debt in the world to repay, this omniscience, compassionate charity that dallied in its giving as if it were, truly a joy, a sadistic joy, to give, and she had to accept the emotional debt Sylvia naturally and instinctively imposed with it.

'I thought you were different,' she said. And immediately added, 'To the other men, I mean,' and immediately added, 'I know you are different, too.'

The need to be alone now with a bottle was overwhelming. Any cheap hotel. Cheap. I showed her the total amount of money I had, the total. She said it wasn't much, not when measured against the future, even if it was American and held its value.

This remark must have brought some response into my eyes. She said she knew a hotel, almost American style, three dollars a night.

It resembled a hotel as a tenement resembles a castle, but it was called the Hotel Napoli, and was the sole income of the old Italian woman who ran the house. She thought I wanted the room for a quick mount, and asked if I'd like her to put a beer in the cooler for me. I said I wouldn't be back down for twenty-four hours. Without emotion she said 'Bravo' and handed me the room key and her gummy jaws collapsed again into each other, in thought or memory or resignation. It was hard to say, but I'd been dismissed.

The room was a respectable stall with a steel-framed bed, an armchair and a chair. There was a cupboard of a washroom. But it also had an air-conditioning unit and an icebox. I asked if Lia might bring back some cheap beer after she'd collected her things from Sylvia's. She said no: that would be cheating Maria, who had already asked me if I wanted beer in the cooler. I had simply misunderstood the language, and a million other things. But I was forgiven, and the beer was promised.

I got some things out of my shoulderbag, got a towel and wrapped it around my neck, took off my shoes and socks, and squatted against the wall facing the jalousied darkened window. Maria knocked and came in and put the beer in the cooler. She said there was another man who once was Irish in the city. He was from Cork, with red hair, and lived on the pavement down by the main telephone office. There was some sickness there, in the head, she said, poor man. Or perhaps I misunderstood. From her bib pocket she took a glass, wiped it again, and handed it to me.

'Ciao, O Senhor.'

'Ciao, Maria.'

'Leila's very beautiful, isn't she, I wonder why she comes here.'

'Ciao, Maria.' And she left, having created and sown mysteries for me to ponder. I spat them out, got my bottle out of the bag, and filled the glass. I had my own mysteries to ponder.

When Lia came back into the room and locked it, the

glass was less than half gone. She barely smiled to see me. Now she looked old, immensely old, wounded eyes, tired and wearied, old and well-wearied of life. She barely smiled to see me. Her belongings were in a slim looking plastic bag. She took a beer and sipped from it, sitting on the far side of the bed. I felt very companionable with her friendship, and went back to my own thoughts. When she said she was going to sleep just a little it had nothing to do with me and I shrugged my shoulders at her. But after she'd taken off her shoes she began to climb, still dressed in uniform jeans and teeshirt, into the bed. I said that monkeys have to endure being monkeys, no matter how clever they are, and especially if they're smart. I had to endure being me, without further comment. But surely she could undress herself and go to bed properly without believing I'd start yodelling and rape her at the first glimpse of tit?

She tried to smile, but her eyes were too old. I raised my glass and closed my eyes. And with the eyes of a betrayed child she stood bowed and sideways to me, undressed herself, and got into bed, normally.

'Bravo.'

I saw her smile then as she pulled the sheet over herself and turned into her sleep.

How long after that to the first sharp movement from the bed I'll never ever know. I was well into my bottle and perhaps the movement had happened before but I'd been too absorbed to notice it. It was an abruptly quick movement of her legs. And then she'd draw her legs closer to herself, and continue sleeping peacefully. The house was quiet, the room was quiet and darkened against the sun, and I was again happy with my bottle and again the legs moved with a frightening punch of movement against the sheet. And again I was utterly sober for seconds while I watched as she pulled her legs up to herself and put her arms around them. This was not going to be a good drunk. I needed a good drunk, but she had frightened me and ruptured it. I thought I was almost sober. Then she murmured, some suppressed noises passed her mouth, and I watched as she squeezed her legs tighter to her and they snapped away and punched and heeled the sheets and went rigidly straight. I eased myself gently down next to her and softly placed my arm around her. Her hands grabbed my arm, between wrist and elbow, and fastened, and began to break my arm. All of her strength was fastened to my arm and it had to break, at any second. But I couldn't stop her. Her power was too great for me, I didn't have the strength. I lost all sensation in my arm and hand. Her legs punched out again and kicked, kicked hard and constantly against my legs. The noises coming from her mouth were broken bits of Portuguese, German, French, English. She grunted, as wild and dangerous as any other animal in combat. But her grip on my arm never eased. And I wished she'd be done with it. Put an end to her illness, leave go my arm and let me nurse, alone, whatever damage she'd done to me. If her fears and demons were so close, so near the surface of her mind, why couldn't she quickly kill them, why was this battle taking so long, why was it so intimately intense and so exclusionary, so selfish. Despite all, I was impatient with her, with her illness, and disappointed with her. I felt I had a right to be callous. All of my instinctive love for her did not extend in any way to her illness. I was impatient and irked by it. She had to end it, and quickly. Yet I lay and endured the smell, the sweat, the kicking, and my lifeless arm limp in her grip.

Time would not move, and there was no respite in my ordeal. She was trembling now. A soft, constant shiver. Then her left leg moved rigidly as steel and raised itself stiffly into the air. She moaned and started to cry in her sleep.

What do people mean when they say that they pray? Do they address their Gods as intimates, whisper mental confidences? What disturbances of mind give them an object of address in the universe? What do they know and understand that I do not? What desert of hopelessness, of panic, of despair, forces them to address, across an infinity of mental space and of physical space, another consciousness in the universe? Is it the ritual, fanatical passion of the gambler believing his intuition is uniquely true and revealed to him, alone, yet he must fanatically bend his entire being, twist his reason, his history, his logic, to justify the hunch?

Then the mad despair at losing. What mad minutiae of ritual was omitted?

I was doing that, praying, willingly, and became more desperate at every infinite moment of loss, was willing to lose more of my rationality into wagering on blind appeals to an addressless universe.

Her hands moved towards her outstretched legs, and she moaned in pain just as she touched it. She raised her body and worked her hands hard about the muscles around and above her knee. And I could say my prayer for random chance to favour me was randomly answered. I moved my body to pull away my limp arm. It was all right, it was unbroken.

In sleep she was massaging her legs. Her breathing was deep, very deep. I reached, grabbed my bottle, and drank directly from it. Relief hit me long before the alcohol. I drank again, more relaxed now, and lay back on the bed. Then consciousness left me. The pain in my arm awoke me. The room was now utterly dark, and Lia was nestled backwards into me and sleeping soundly. Gently I slipped from the bed, got to the cooler, got a beer, and cracked it open. It was delicious, and I guzzled it all and cracked open another. This I could sip in peace.

It was the middle of the night. I lit a cigarette, pulled on it, and blew out the smoke. So much aesthetic, drugged joy; so many unformed and unfocused tensions dissolved themselves in the delicious smoke. I sipped my beer in the darkness.

Such brief moments of peace can be all of happiness to me. It is here in these quiet intervals that I find my home, my home unto me, in this existence. Home, incommunicado. The treasured beauty of being at one with myself, and not being dispersed and lost to myself. The world was silent, and the dawn was far, far away. In this niche I was safe.

She whispered my name, my recently bestowed name, in the darkness, and asked me, already in the manner of a wife of long standing, what time was it and what was I doing up.

The tropical night was freezing. She pulled the sheets with her, left the bed and came to squat beside me. She sipped my beer and took a drag on my cigarette, then turned her body and settled herself up into my lap.

'Why did you want to leave me?' she asked. 'I saw your eyes when you gave your passport to the soldier. You loved me then.'

'He was the immigration officer.'

She laughed. 'Oh no, no, he was just a soldier. He asked for your passport just for the bribe the gringos always put there.' And she lightly laughed again, and then kissed me. 'Gringo!'

It was so easy to make her joyful, and so joyful to look at her joyfulness. I began to tell her a story. And the scepticism that immediately surrounded the beatific smile dappled her beauty. I said that when I was hungry I went to eat. Not always my palate's nor my heart's desire, but whatever I could manage to quench my appetite and take it away from my concerns. I didn't squat outside restaurants and gawk at the diners inside. I would never allow myself to betray my poverty to others. In the manner that I have never been able to read or watch pornography, because I find it demeaning to squat outside and gawk like a miser or an inadequate in front of a restaurant. I have more vanity than that; I can only beg in private. And this honesty is also another kind of vanity, of preening. I am so dishonest to myself, and to everyone else, that I can admit my own regrets, but only in order to appear bigger and greater than they; and that is not at all possible: otherwise I would not be writing this.

Her fingers and lips were playing about my face.

And yes, I loved you then, loved you as if I had already loved you all of my life. But that hadn't been so. I had missed you, missed you and others, in my youth and adulthood, missed 'the wine, the women, and the glory, all in one sitting' many, many times. And now I am in these years where those losses return with spite to jeer and haunt old age with all of the many things it missed in its youth and prime. And the words are bitter and dirty and sick with regret.

'You are in your prime,' she said, and her body rose lovingly against me, 'You are a man in the prime of his strength.'

And immediately there was a strength in me.

'A man in the prime of this character and strength,' she said. And all I had wanted to say, that my best years were past, that hers were yet to come, that I could not cope with life and I wanted my life to end, these were mumbled to myself or whispered to her through my fretting hands. I had always thought that when hope dies, life soon followed. But that is not the case. I lived on, into a vacancy of life, and wholly unnoticed by death. I had come to die in the heat and warmth of this beautiful country, this country of my dreams. I, who did not know which other way to turn now, in life had turned every way in every sense, every manner, and always found before me a stone wall that curved away from me in its darkness, but still imprisoned me in the confines of an empty, unwanted space of existence. 'Wine, women, and glory' become the stale and mirthless jokes of the callow, and of fools. And the transparency of all irked me. There was no purchase into meaning in life.

When I turned to take her in our first communion her eyes again reminded me of the mountain cat, and I noticed how white the sheet was against the golden brown of her naked skin.

And I noticed that she favoured one of my arms over the other, was most gentle with it, and kissed it often.

After the most sensitive, most solitary, most truculent moment of communion she asked if I were happy now. To please her I said yes, and she tightened magically on me.

I heard ghosts in other languages, remembered other gestures of other manners in other realms. All had turned to the substance of shadows, and disappeared into the empty daylight of morning. When I most needed them, as reality, or even as illusions. Now all I wanted was to sit gently against this wall in a distant dark room, drink beer, smoke cigarettes, and hold fast onto the night. And at these moments to understand that participation in life also requires, to a vital degree, a suspension of disbelief.

'Come to eat with me,' she said, 'Come. Later you can sit alone and drink.'

Outside, in the light of the hallway, I saw again how haggard and old her eyes had become. And I wondered how old and derelict I appeared to her.

Maria looked worried when she saw 'Leila's' face, and looked worriedly at me. She looked more worried when we said we were going to eat at the Central Bar, and said she would cook for us, and for less than the Central Bar's rate. And Lia said all right, but we'd walk about for half an hour. And Maria said I must take a gun the streets were so dangerous. And from her bib she produced the little monstrous thing. It was snub-nosed Taurus 38, with a beautiful wooden handle, and fired hollow-nosed, dum-dum bullets. It was an instrument of war. I said if the scene was really so heavy perhaps we had better get helicopter gunship back-up. She wasn't amused, and insisted I hold it in my pocket with the safety off. Then she noticed the massive bruising on my arm, faltered in her speech for a moment, and said 'Leila' must eat a lot of pasta tonight, pasta with butter and garlic. And still she hurried on in her speech, as if to block some persistent inner voice of alarm, and talked nonsensically about a recipe she'd brought with her from Italy when she was a sixteen-year-old postal bride, for a middle-aged Italian who wanted a girl from the Old Country, the stupid schmuck, with Brazil full of the world's most beautiful women, and he was beer-bellied and flabby and lazy with self-indulgent conceit weak and unpleasant in his big plump mama's boy's face. And, and, and ...

I had to back away from the torrent. The effort of catching one word in five and guessing at the others from her gestures and facial expressions was wearying me. I put the bloody gun, catch off, into my pocket, and ushered Lia out. Maria, still blabbering, bolted the door behind us.

Outside, in the delicious cold scent of the night's air, I put the safety catch back on and emptied the shells from the chamber. Carrying a gun instantly kills the human instinct for danger, the human instinct of self-preservation. It bestows delusions of God-like grandeur. If you use the gun, and someone shoots back at you, you immediately feel a sense of unfairness, that he should have a gun too, and be more adept in its use than you. It takes a lot of murderously noisy work to learn how to hit a barn door, any barn door, from thirty paces, with one of these elephant-kick, arm-breaking revolvers. Then you meet someone who uses it like a water-pistol. It's so unfair, and it writes *finis* to the dreams of the little boy within.

I gave Lia the shells, and stuffed the gun down the inside of my sock.

I love the empty night streets. You can see the city's architecture in relief against the night's sky, see the dreams in the facades, see the hurt rupture in the streets, and sense and partake of all the sweat and blood and energy of the long-dead craftsmen. Sounds are distinct and pure, and linger in the air to be recognised. Even the oldest, most broken street, in the most broken slum, becomes an antique, mellow with sad memories, and as quietly anxious as a charming old woman to tell you of her radiant childhood, her beautiful adolescence, the hard struggle, the scars, the wounds, and the glory, and the gradual decline into the silent wretchedness of abandoned, disrespected old age. I caught Lia trying to suppress her laughter as she regarded me daydreaming merrily to myself. I had to laugh too, and we tricked with each other, and shouted into the still night, and I chased her, always just an inch away from a supernatural doom, along the resounding, cobbled street.

At the corner she slowed and hushed me to silence. Here was where the man who once was Irish, from Cork, lived. But she did not believe him. Once when a sailor had been kind to her she had telephoned for a job in a different city. But the questions overwhelmed her. She realised she didn't know her date of birth because she had never celebrated her birthday, never knew it was her feast day, and didn't know her mother's maiden name. So she hadn't even gotten to fill out an application over the phone, and the stupid bitch at the other end had been insulting and acted cool and clever, because she had all of this information readily available about herself, and thought that this was proof of a bright and shining intelligence. She was only a pimp, the cold and dumb bitch, processing people for her employers. And too dumb to know that. That was why she had the job.

Coming out, the man who once was Irish, from Cork, held out his hand for the loose change. The coins for the phone-box were of too little value ever to buy anything, unless you collected a great horde of them. She still had the money from the sailor, and she asked the man who once was Irish, from Cork, and who spoke Portuguese Portuguese, if he'd teach her an English lesson from her grammar for five US dollars. He shouted at her abusively, and used ancient words, and dribble came to his mouth and madness in his eyes, and he railed at her that he was no fucking agent of British imperialism from inside the pale, that she should be proud of her native 'tongue' and maintain it as her cultural heritage, and teach it properly to her children, and he'd be shagging damned before he'd ever teach anyone English and undermine their cultural identity for the nefarious — he stuttered on his own venom and repeated the word, the fucking nefarious ends of British imperialism.

So she didn't really believe he was Irish and could speak English, and all this shouting was just a cover. He was a stuck-up Portuguese bum who hadn't made it and was pretending to be Irish.

When we rounded the corner there were more than a dozen lost souls sleeping in the alcove of the telephone exchange. The one Lia pointed out didn't need that service. I had never before seen red hair streaked with grey, as his was, and he looked bitterly old, and looked bitter and vindictive in his sleep. But even more, there was a thin, silver steel chain fastened to his wrist. On the other end of the chain was a bright-eyed mongrel dog eyeing us suspiciously while his master slept. Even street-beggars were afraid of being mugged in their sleep. Or this one was. When the dog saw the dollar bill he allowed me to approach, and I slipped it into the sleeping man's outstretched hand. Then I assured Lia that I knew that he was the man who once was Irish, from Cork. The dog squatted back down on his master's rump, and napped.

Further up the street we came to the historic Central Bar.
It was in the hotel of this bar, for it was that way arranged,
that General O'Leary, having arrived in Itaqui after
escaping at Pernambuco from the convict ship bringing him
from Bermuda to Australia, months after General John
Mitchell had declined to break his promise to the British
and had returned aboard the convict ship to the dismay and
boos of the free Brazilians, that General John O'Leary had
had 147 women (one hundred and forty seven) in one night,
a real Irishman, seven and a half women per hour.

She learned this information in one of the hotel's
bedrooms on a blue plaque put there by the city
government of the time to commemorate the event. But the
bed was gone. A sympathiser, a sympathiser of Irish
Republicanism in France had bought it, and it was now in
the French Savoie museum.

Every reference was so bizarre, everything so out of tilt,
fiction given the pulse beat of truth by a sailor's joke on his
home country in a hotel bedroom. Seven and a half an hour
worked out at nineteen hours, a long night, but Brazilians,
like myself, find such irritating arithmetic a graceless thing
devoid of the life pulse and splendour of art. And so they
junk it as missing the point, as it does. And having come to
this beautiful country to die, I knew I had come home, and
my death will be easy and peaceful, among friends, and, so
to speak, relatives, relatives of blood and beer and amazing
feats.

The shuttered doors of the Central Bar were stacked
away on each side of the entrance. There was no music, but
the noise of camaraderie filled the huge bar. There were free
wide spaces between the tables, and around two tables
pushed together in the exact middle of the bar were the
Dutch sailors from the ship I'd travelled on. On their laps

were huge Gorgons of women, black, white and mulatto.
How these guys were going to get their fantasies off on
these waddles of fat was, like prayer, beyond my
comprehension. To have sex with any of these women
would be an act of the most pure, most selfless,
philanthropic love. No way could they arouse lust, or even
curious desire, in a normal heterosexual male, even if he'd
been denied women for the last twenty years in the French
Foreign Legion. He'd turn around and re-enlist. To mount
any of these women, aside from requiring the most blind act
of faith, literally, would also require the aid of a forklift
truck. It would be easier to tip your toes while leaning over
a barrel. I hoped O'Leary, after three years in prison, had
had better luck. The whites were the obscene colour of lard,
lard that was cemented with powder and gashes of rouge in
front of an aged photograph of someone else in a dark
room. Each was at least old enough to be the grandmother
of even the oldest sailor present. I understood why the
sailors were sick with drunkenness, and did not condemn
them for it. It was an appalling sight and I was shocked and
very glad I had agreed to eat at Maria's. At Maria's, with
Maria who had aged with pragmatism and grace.

I wanted to take a table near the entrance, to turn my
back on the inferno of vanity and despair. Lia said we had
to go to the table, for a while. She had to acknowledge
Sylvia and the others. The Dutch looked at Lia, at me, and
their national inferiority complex took on an extra spin. The
Gorgon who was Sylvia at once examined me closely with
her brazen acquisitive eyes looking for any weakness to
probe. And immediately she knew I had a gun, and where
it was. She became canny and suspicious. She asked Lia to
tell her again where she had met the rich gentleman. To my
bewilderment she addressed Lia as Leticia. Lia said I had
been the Professor of English and German at the Irish

University of Cork, that I had come here to rest and teach a little at the Catholic University, and she had met me as she used to meet the sailors, helping them to make it safely and inexpensively from the docks to the city in return for a fee. It was better than whoring, she said, and smiled a most honestly vicious smile at Sylvia. Sylvia went coy, like a juggernaut trying to shimmy without going out of control, held onto the table to stop the slight inertia of her movement toppling her across the width of the bar, and most grandly asked me if I might occasionally give her an English lesson. Lia said I charged six US dollars an hour and accepted bookings only with payment a week in advance. For the second time in my life, the second time in twenty-four hours, I prayed to the Universe.

I abhor violence, but Lia was going to suffer, when I got her alone, a most severe, untempered scolding.

Then, dear Jesus, the Gorgon heaved forth a mound of dollar bills from some long neglected cranny on her person. I froze. Lia said I was now fully booked for next week. For that kindness I instantly forgave her her scolding, and wondered how much the local whiskey was.

Lia reached, took the money, placed it into my limp hand and called me O Senhor — Sir. I bowed stiffly to Sylvia, said noon, this day next week, at a location Lia would arrange.

Lia turned me, and we walked arm in arm to a table at the entrance of the twice historic Central Bar. I asked a smiling waiter to bring us two beers, and Lia asked where had I learned this formal Portuguese Portuguese. Later, child, later.

The beer came in pleasant litre bottles, deeply chilled, and I have never tasted beer of such exquisite flavour. The two bottles cost a dollar and I knew I was being ripped off. But I decided not to protest.

Lia said that twelve bottles of this for teaching Sylvia bad

German was fair recompense. And then she laughed, in a world of her own, and her small fists pummelled the table in an intense victory tattoo. I knew that from now on I would never do anything to incur Lia's wrath, nor even her slightest displeasure, nor to anyone else so deeply capable of wreaking such cold blooded malice and vengeance.

I was filled with a supernatural, a supreme happiness. I told Lia a little story, of the time I sold Belize driving licenses and university degrees, of my own design and watermark, through the mail to deserving yuppies. During my research I browsed into works of economics, and obediently followed their precepts. My business declined. Literally I couldn't give the things away. And out of exasperated mischievousness I increased my prices to astronomical levels. I sold everything I could produce. And thus learned that there is a class of person who cannot believe they are getting genuine value unless they are being unmercifully ripped off.

I said we would have to increase the price to twelve dollars. We had, so to speak, overheads to consider. Sylvia had received a once-off discount on account of friendship. But the price was now twelve dollars. Lia examined me, silently, and then nodded her wise young head. Twelve dollars.

I had another long bottle of the cold, glorious beer, and Lia bought me a bottle of the noble, local whiskey. The tropical night sky was a shabby, an unwashed, weak blue. I wondered about the midnight skies in local places I had learned to love well in this world. Perhaps some night in the future, in some other place, I would wonder about this night. But no, there wasn't time enough, life enough, left for that. Not enough life left for that. There was nothing sobering or melancholic in this thought. Just a pinch of fear worried itself quickly alive in my stomach, like a maggot. I had spent so much time in my life forgetting this time would come, or pretending I could postpone it or escape it. Not enough life left to think about a future. So much gone. So much sweat and hardship for the virtual durance of getting the material necessities, day by vanishing day, day after day, no life at all visible in their passing but endurance, forbearance, and the nurturing of small dreams of tomorrow, some tomorrow, until there was here: not enough time for dreams of tomorrow. My money did not accrue to me as a surplus, but was scurried away at the expense of proper necessities, was very 'little when measured against the future', even if that were only a day. No surplus wealth of any kind had accrued to me. I had lived so long, to see the revelation of communism's practice, and the world's rejection of communism, and its return to the free marketing of goods and people, like ancient times. I had lived too long. Already the streets everywhere were dangerous, like ancient times, as people turned themselves back to prey and predator, the commands and imperatives of the jungle, as if this were all that economic science, or all science, any science, could teach us. And truly communism was foul and tragic, like Dickensian times, and I was further lost and confused in my own contradictions.

I came back to the present and finished my beer.

'Home?' she asked, and for a moment the word and the concept bewildered me. Home? I thought she was inquiring after my musings, was asking if I had been thinking of that place where I had come from. But that wasn't home; and then my mind was fully back in the present.

Home, yes, it would be nice to go home, and with many smiles and bows to the Gorgons and the Dutch we wandered away into the night.

At the telephone exchange we stopped. The dollar bill was gone from the hand of the man who once was Irish, from Cork. But no thief could have stolen it from under the nose of the dog. Lia approached and petted the dog, and praised his courage. The beast thought this was no more than his due, and hardly even wagged his tail. I abused him for this, and called him a dog who no more than once was Irish, from Cork. His ears peaked and his feet stepped slightly on his master's haunches. Lia petted and cooed him back to docility. Then we strolled away. After a moment we started to laugh, convulsively, for many reasons. Then we settled and strolled back richly to our residence; Maria's Hotel Napoli. Maria unbolted the door and let us in. She re-bolted it and immediately asked me for the gun. And stupidly, leaning over to take it from my sock, I pulled it free, put it to my head, shouted Ah! and pulled the trigger. Almost as the hammer sprung Lia roared in an agony of despair and her fist punched my face. I stumbled back and she followed, kicking and punching at me, and crying and snarling. Maria tried to pull her away. She refused and came back to me and put her arms around me and sobbed. She stepped away, crying, and looked at me, and hit me less hard than before and pulled me to her and cried against me. She kept saying, mumbling, something, and I finally recognised the word: arrogance, arrogance, arrogance. I said I was sorry, many times. I tried to hold her but she elbowed my arms away, then put her arms around me again and held me to her.

After a while I looked to Maria, but got no sympathy. I had to wait until the crying subsided, wait long after it appeared to have stopped, then let my eyes plead with Maria again. I kept saying I was sorry. But I was aware of the unforgivable nature of my stupidity, and the desolation it led to. This was not even a new, a novel experience to me. I knew that then, with humbling, pellucid clarity.

Maria finally came, with many murmurs and coaxings, to

take Lia into her arms and bring her towards where I supposed the dining room was. I said I'd go upstairs to my room. I said I'd wait. I said I'd pay a week's rent later today. No one paid any attention.

I went upstairs, felt ashamed and cowardly that I didn't have the brazenness to recover the fallen bottle of whiskey, and didn't have a bright little story to camouflage my persistent inability to understand another person's intimate and sacred reality, and, sometimes, my intimate, even if casual, place therein. My mind began thinking about making up such a decorous little story.

Once I closed the room door I began to feel differently. I began to discount my losses. I thought about turning the key in the door, to exercise a little spite and to pre-empt any change. But there were a few beers, and a little whiskey remaining in the bottle, to be drunk yet. I settled down to that indulgent sorrow. Life was really out of control and I decided not to lock the door. At the time I thought that was magnanimous, that it showed I was not totally wrapped-up in myself. And for all the wrong reasons, that was true, then.

Half an hour later I knew she wouldn't come, but I still didn't want to sleep so it really wasn't necessary to lock the door. A little while later sleep began to gather rapidly around me, and it probably wasn't necessary anyway to lock it in a place like Maria's. I went to sleep.

When I awoke I was alone. Beautiful sunlight was streaming in the window and particles of dust hovered in the beam. For some moments all was pleasant, then the fear coughed to life in my stomach. Another day of durance in this world. I knew the day ahead so well, its uselessness to me, that it was already a used and a soiled, a secondhand day. Just to get my breathing easier I showered. The shower was a simple tap set high in the wall in the washroom, and the water came out at ambient temperature; lukewarm. The longer I stayed the nicer it became, and I had to consciously avoid drinking the gushing, embracing water. I dried myself and squatted down naked on the bed, dimly aware that I was enjoying this existence, enjoying it deeply. I took a beer.

The day was out there; waiting. People moving with purpose; people who did not expect the world to notice their misfortunes, to feel guilt or pity for them. People who would struggle and kick for an extra hour in the day, an extra day in their lives. People who were determined, as determined as toughened soldiers in battle to do what they do to survive. In them there is always the sharp and angry terror of soldiers in combat for their very lives. In all the uniforms of work, from banker to beggar. The practises of battle are intimately known to them, the drudgery, the bravery, the suffering; the human needs unremitting in the very face of abundant death; and the common brute brutality demanded if they are not to fall in the insanity. They take their coffee breaks, and laugh, never really on furlough. For all of their lives, a sweaty and muddy and bloody ordeal. Enemies found and friends lost, all in the same uniform of struggle in the relentless business of the world. Planting seed for food, caring for animals for slaughter; the transport, administration, jurisdiction, regulation, enforcement, sanitation, burial, servicing; of food and waste, all the wherewithal of human life, processing humans in a harsh shuttlecock of producers and consumers, soldier to soldier, under the same uniform. And more. All that must be done, day by day. The battle of the treadmill to keep society moving while the soldiers go around and around, are born, reared and die. Out there, clear in the daylight, the hustle of constant battle. The numbing, military regularity and predictability of it all, of bloody life and death. It's never personal, this activity of the species.

When you leave this battle, for any reason, re-entering it is a terrifying experience, a screechless horror of awe and numbing fear that you must fall in and bear up. I had not the courage. The only options are the asylum of broken down cowardice and the fate of deserters. The treadmill grinds on. Nothing personal. Then you are aware of the sky, the sun, the galaxy, the cosmos. The labour of brains and sweat to produce wherewithal for the worked species on this rock of a planet seems hilarious, and then harsh, and frightening, and incomprehensible.

There's no mixing with the species without a total suspension of bewilderment and disbelief.

I found my sedatives and swallowed two. Normally they require sugar and caffeine to become fully active, but alone they would cool me enough to face Maria, anyway. Or maybe they wouldn't. Normally they give the placid serenity of the condemned, and the doomed, and a dimmed understanding that the last eternal second will not be so beguiled. I waited a little while, then dressed and went downstairs, the first skirmish of the day.

'Bom dia a senhora.'

But she smiled warmly back and told me to help myself to coffee and food in the diningroom. She chatted pleasantly as she showed the plates of egg, cheese, meat, fruit, all the ample proportions of a Brazilian breakfast. The next feed was late afternoon, and dinner was after sunset. Then she said, as if it were of hushed, momentous importance, that of course Leila was angry with me and had gone away. I knew this was an old woman's mischievous lie. Lia's plastic bag and its possessions were in my room. But I hadn't actually looked, I hadn't checked it this morning. It was wholly forgotten until I heard this threat.

I said I was happy to see the last of the little girl. I paid out a week's rent, and sat down to enjoy my food. I hoped by my manner to show that she was dismissed. She half went, but loitered, and said Leila had gone to the Square Lisboa, just up the street facing the Central Bar. I tossed my head and threw a waving hand towards her and set about feeding myself. Silently she left. I would have liked her company, had it been silent, or had it been co-operative and not so innately manipulative. But anyway I ate well with a pure and luscious appetite. It was such a contradiction. My life was a failure and had no further progress available. Only death would seal up the misbegotten, the badly handled, the useless and redundant life. Yet I ate as if preparing for a siege.

Maria came in with a plate of peeled bananas doused in sugar and set them in front of me. She told me also to drink some milk from the jug. It was special milk. Then she sat opposite me and looked towards the window. Silently. But not for long.

It would be a convenience, she said, for many girls, although the men would benefit too, if there were postal brides nowadays. The sugared bananas and the special milk were doing wonders to my mouth. I nodded.

But not to Europe, she said, not to send the girls to Europe. They were cold, hard people there; they liked pain, bad weather, drudgery. They wallowed in hardship, endurance, the grunt, the struggle, and the hurt. From this they emerge like Titans, crucified but triumphant. She shook her head. It was the only time I ever saw silent, meditative thought control her. Then she looked at me and said, with a laugh that was a little too hearty for her age:

'We know, don't we.'

And she said it with all the histrionic panache of the little actress within her. She was looking at me, but not intrusively, as I finished the last banana and the glass of special milk.

'This is a new world,' she said, 'for us, for Europeans. It's always rough and dangerous in a new world. A new world, but with no Ellis Islands, no Dictation Tests, no humiliation; we don't have to bend the knee or doff the cap. This is a glorious new world. Glorious. Glorious.'

I didn't answer. She began to clear away the table.

'Leave Europe behind you,' she said, calling me familiarly by the name Lia had given me, 'Leave it behind here,' she said, tapping on her head. 'No one cares why you came, why you had to come. Leave it behind.'

I began to rise from the table, and nodded that I understood.

'She's not a little girl. You've had her, and you know you've had a full woman. She has a passion for you, and can express it. What can you do? Behind your European facade? Behave like a child? But I know you're a good man. Not like the European schmuck I married.'

I laughed, that old women can say this about men they've lived with for dozens of years, and probably cried, even mourned, when they died. I only knew she was old, eccentric and humorous, and brimful of anecdotal knowledge. She said she was life-long tired of lies and convention, polite and otherwise, that she was the first to know that children and the mentally young must play, must scrape their knees, break bones, must scream their presence into the universe, and must hold the passions of their loves and hates with all the strength of mules. And that these are a pure and genuine source of the nostalgia of later times. That it is all much, much better, even at its worst, than never playing at all. She was still blabbering, to the wall or to me, when I went out onto the streets.

The avenues of Itaqui were built in the seventeenth century. They face directly onto the sea and catch the prevailing easterly winds. Even the streets off the avenues catch eddies of this breeze before it rises above the heat of the land. The French builders believed in permanence. The buildings are made of the same stone as the streets. Time has worked on them all. They have an air of art, of inspiration, like a picture reflecting human ambiguity, like a story in the telling being well told. About the streets there are stone benches, and you can sit in one and know you rub off life as much as the armies of France, the Netherlands, Britain, Portugal, wore off their strength fighting through the centuries for this city, until the Brazilians finally took it and held it in peace ever since. It is a city that tells you, like all of South America, to take your happiness much more seriously than your sorrows. Your life's production of happiness must some day overwhelm the desolation of your death. A most solid, material city, imperious and secure in its timelessness, it liberates and celebrates the human spirit, like a painting or a story well told.

Sitting in one of the broad-benched, broad-backed seats, I tried again to recall my attempt on death. Somehow it is known that this act cannot be individually remembered. Under medical hypnosis, under truth-serum narcotics, those who have made an attempt on death cannot remember the final details of their assault. They remember walking to the bridge, but not falling; squeezing the trigger, and nothing else; swallowing the tablets, but not falling asleep. The brain cannot understand these events, and there are no traces of their memory in it. The brain believes in the second law of thermodynamics, the law that determines even the death of the universe, but the brain cannot make sense of its own demise, it being so clever and, oh, so wise. And hence it ignores the direct extinction of itself. It does not understand how to compute this, and returns the fact as an abstract idea of probability and possibility. It is neither. It is as inevitable as a finger of hot metal now erupting through your head at a speed greater than the speed of sound. You'll never remember it.

Sitting under the sun in that most charming and magical little city, sitting in a centuries-old bench, smoking my aesthetic cigarette, I could remember the events of my assault on death, the hungry rush for it, and then the re-emergence of life, as it re-formed its concerns and my personal response to them, as my personality re-emerged to the only form my brain would allow: me. Though I had to relearn some details about my body and mentality and attitude, unexpected weaknesses, unexpected strengths, unexpected oddities. I had to relearn them because they were there, given, part of me. Yet by a simple measurement of time I know life went away. I just cannot recall or remember it when it wasn't there. Not at all like sleep. There is always a felt continuation during and after sleep. Sleep is living, often it is intense and satisfied living. In sleep I've had some near-life experiences, the only ones I've ever had. In dreams, yes.

Practised, vibrant, fluent, masterful life. Not the paltry work for paltry rewards that permit paltry existences that most beasts of burden like humans endure. Because their sensible brains, their brains that have no structural nor architectural difference from Michaelangelo's or Einstein's, and capable of receiving the same furnishings, with the same information, their sensible brains believe that miserable life is better than unimprovable death. All brains are innately capable of the same sublimity of the most superb art and science, despite visible evidence everywhere to the contrary, and all brains are susceptible to the same constraints, the same cramping, the same diminution, the same malfunctioning, the same wounding, as the most miserable case in any ward in any asylum; irreparably broken, maimed, and wasted. With just the slightest insight into my own condition, I knew to which end of the spectrum I tended.

Sitting in that ancient bench in the beautiful, fresh day, I decided to give death another try. To watch for the opportunity. Because it is not like going to sleep. The jerk and the snapping of life is not at all like that. Again I thought about what they might do with my body afterwards. The vanity of the brain interfered and made me feel squeamish, tried to frighten me, about hands handling my body, rolling it downstairs, pitching it into a grave, or pushing it into a furnace, pulling out the roasted bones and the quick pounding of them to sand under a massive weight of steel. Only then, when I contemplated myself as grains of sand, did the brain suddenly retire, unable to locate itself or its vanity anywhere there. The me my brain always saw had slipped away, unnoticed. Life ought to have been wonderful, I know. It wasn't.

After all the pain and terror — everyone does it with the slowest, greatest terror, the slowest, greatest sadness, and the unbelievable sob that breaks, the last sob with the last thought as consciousness disappears is Jesus let it all end forever and forever, and screams, forever, forever: I cannot endure —

I cannot endure.

— after doing the act, of acting fully contrary to nature, the entire thrust of life, after the final investment of all beliefs and all bitter bravery, I was still, unforgivably, alive. I had done it. All and more than was necessary to end my life, and I became unforgivably alive. I sank into a depression of unquenchable wild white eyes forever open forever staring. Then I realised I was detached from life; a dead man on furlough, still just like everyone else.

The life of the street bustled around me, and there was palpable happiness in it. People were relaxed, at ease with themselves and with each other. This was the lineage of rebels. There was an easy and proud, happy tilt to every head. The mixed lineage — of the courageous who left Europe and made a life for themselves here, the strong, the nimble, and the wily, and of those who had survived the passage from Africa and the generations of slavery, of the indigenous people who survived the invading, rapacious onslaught — was blended from these, and more. There are numerous versions of Brazilians, but there is no prototype, no stock figure. No old Etonian, no cloth cap, no predictable Hans, no drunken Paddy, no wily Frog. Yet many recognised my gringo foreignness as I strolled up the street, and smiled at me and said 'Bom dia!'

The Square Lisboa is a park sunk six feet below street level. It is hundreds of years old and cobbled walkways section it into triangular gardens. There are stone benches along the walkways and shady alcoves along the bottom of the walls. Except on Saturdays and Sundays, Indians in loincloths come direct from the forests to sell leather goods, wooden sculptures, and illegal alcohol. People stroll about to take their ease, as if from another century, and schoolgirls mingle with business girls at the lemonade stands. Streetboys sell tiny plastic cups of coffee from long metal vacuum cylinders slung to their shoulders like stovepipes and offer sachettes of sugar from their pockets to businessmen and tourists and common idlers.

I saw Lia. She was deep in chatter and laughter with Sylvia and the other Gorgons, and some other girls as lovely and blossoming as herself. She saw me, and something of a quick stricture came upon her face and movements. But only for a second. I went back to street level, walked about until I was overhead the alcove where they laughed and rotated in and out like children, and squatted about. I sat myself on the parapet to listen. They knew I was there and carried on regardless, salaciously. But they were, all of them, in chatter and laughter, most assuredly, under the entire sway of the little child within. As if growing-up, for them, had been a waste of time, or was merely another kind of fancy-dress make-up.

The fleet was gone and the women were counting their gold and recounting their nights. Some of the sailors had fallen in love, some had proposed marriage, some deranged specimens had offered to bring them to Europe. The girls laughed and shouted and pleaded with each other to go on with their stories. Yara was as young and as beautiful as Lia. She said she'd had six men twice, on short-times. When the first one went back to the bar he boasted of how good it had been. The second did the same. And when she had finished the sixth, the first had talked himself into some fantasy and had to have her again. So she doubled the price and told him she had a baby and the baby had no Papa, and she had no Mama or Papa; all alone in the world; and she wanted to go to school and study and make a respectable life for herself and her little baby. Maybe even go to Europe, someday.

The girls were going ooh! and aah! and then they whooped and shrieked and fell about laughing and changed places in some ritual about the alcove.

The man gave her a hundred dollars, but then fucked her so hard she thought he was going to split her in two. But she had the others, a hundred a go, two minutes each and each was done. Just put her hand down and tickled their balls and off they came, presto! presto! presto! presto! presto!

The girls shouted and yipped and cheered. And the amazing stories went on. Some sailors had paid exactly to the cent, some had double or trebled the agreed price, some had tried to weasel out. But ample money had been left behind, and today was Fiesta Time. There were oddities of behaviour, of sailors sucking toes and other things, that I didn't want to hear about. I went back into the Square and found a place where Lia could see me. When she noticed me again she ignored my silent, mouthed greeting. I sat back to endure, for a while.

I was thinking of a car parked in the moorlands of Yorkshire with the engine running, and the hiss of carbon monoxide entering the cabin. And the hellish, maddening noise of the engine that whined and rose and rose and became excruciating and shrieked and was intolerable to life or death.

Then I saw Sylvia arise and waddle towards me. Someone was making sure that I suffered today. She was the most smarmy, uncouth lout I have ever spoken to, and I include a breath-taking gallery. She wanted her English lesson. Right here. Now. No, not in a bar.

'This is my hand,' with the appropriate gesture, is how they begin the teaching of English to speakers of other languages. Repeated endlessly. This is my leg, this is my head, this is my left hand, that is your hand. And finally, with the maximum amount of distrust, and with an ego trying hard to disguise itself, she timidly mimicked me. It is just a slow accretion of small habits, of words and images and movement, a lot of drudgery, and no mental leaps, until bits of language accrue in memory, and you must keep it mobile, and you must have stubborn motivation, and you must practise it as wantonly as a child. But Sylvia knew better. Sylvia wanted to apply cleverness and intellect where dumb obedience and dumb acceptance and active mimicking was required. Thus most of the lesson-time was wasted in useless digressions before anyone but I could have understood a simple sentence from her mouth. I was drenched in sweat. We had made immense, positive progress and I smiled at her, mistakenly, and she saw the truth. I tried to leave.

'The climate of Europe is cold?' she said.

'Yes. Frozen.'

'Ice and cold and fog,' she harried. I shrugged.

'Who emigrates to Europe?' she asked, 'Who wants to live there, in Europe, nowadays?'

Her angle of approach was perfect. She was placing me against a false background in a false row. Only brazenness, a dog's brazenness, can do this.

'Tell me,' she said, and repeated the question.

'Nao sei, Sylvia,' I said humbly, and tried to smile more sincerely than before.

'You don't know!!' she said, 'You don't even know that??'

'I'm sorry, Sylvia,' I said, giving raw meat to a starving dog.

'What do you mean, "I'm sorry, Sylvia",' she asked, 'What does that mean?' And this was going to be the beginning of a torment.

'Read my lips, Sylvia,' and she froze.

Did these harridans ever need Women's Lib? And now, under its flag, they parade their ignorance as female emancipation, and rush to the fore of every group.

'Eh?' she said, with dumb spite curling on her nether lip. 'Eh, what do you mean ...?'

Morally, I might have been losing the skirmish, but at least I could still keep the bloody dogs in check.

I stood up, bowed, shook her hand, smiled, excused myself, and headed directly for the Central Bar. But she knew she had the power to make any day of mine a shabby day. She had this immense, primitive power. Even the effort of being vulgar to her would distort any day of mine, distract and pollute my run of private thought; occupy my mind like an invading army, just as she was doing now. And I could not reciprocate.

Sylvia's cunning instinct now knew she could irk and pester me at will, and almost with impunity. Once the bitch got her nose into that scent nothing, short of me rolling on the ground and exposing my genitals, would pacify her.

I asked for a coffee and a glass of water and tried hard to smile in response to the barman's smile. The paradox of my life. Defeated by inferiors, but since they won, I suppose that makes them my betters. But my brain can't really believe that. I've lived like a beast in the field. Looking back, if ever, for the dumb pleasure of nostalgia. Looking forward, vaguely, dimly, in darkness. The taste of the moment had to be all. If the circumstances didn't suit I never had the strength to change them. So I moved on. Because it is necessary to keep the sultry, envious dogs in check every day, day after day, or remove them from the scene. But anyway I should not have chosen to be in a place where the dogs needed to be kept in check. Thus I forever yielded ground to the dogs of my life. I lacked their primordial force, their territoriality, their undiminished primordiality, bellowing, bestial, implacable, and triumphant. They were in their element now, as fully at home as they would have been in their element a hundred thousand years ago, in the offal-eating society and business life of the forest and the cave.

They came in all together, in an almost unbroken line, with a group swag to their approach, a collective will, the centre of attention, like a band of desperadoes recently unhorsed, their gait rolling and short against the flatness of the earth, like so many, so far unprovoked, hooligans, Sylvia centrally leading the rest and the young women outriders, some almost straggling, unsure, behind. I turned and looked away. They passed with a heel of their bodies scouting about the tables, with a tumult of their presence, and a new atmosphere arising in the change of the air in the bar. In the mirror I saw Yara was the last. And as she airily and coyingly passed by me, I felt a little hand quickly grip and squeeze my left buttock. I groaned, loudly, in nervousness, and heard a delighted giggle from Yara as she went to the back of the bar with the rest of the gang. I heard the chairs being drawn out; and the ease as the controlled stampede ebbed and settled down.

I waited for the last straggler to show. The bar reorganised itself to a subdued accommodation with the presence of the maidens, with the dispersed atmosphere. I asked for another coffee, hoping that the caffeine would give a buzz to the sedative.

'Where's your girlfriend today?' the barman asked.

'I don't know yet,' I answered, lying, surprised that a

stranger was keeping tabs on me.

'I think she's in the Square,' he said.

I looked around. At the back of the bar Yara, with a bright, tropical smile, bent her arms and raised her fists to her shoulders and her body shook in a Go! Go! Go! signal. I had to smile. I swallowed the coffee and went.

It was a long, long walk from the time I felt her noticing me to my stomach-tightening arrival at the alcove. She was sitting so solemn-faced, solemn and severe, her chin hard and tilted. And there, next to her feet, was her orange plastic bag of possessions.

I sat beside her and said again: 'I'm sorry. I apologise.'

'It's all right,' she said, 'I understand you.'

I was looking across the Square, above the burnished, thatch-coloured roofs of the French colonial buildings, at the sky, the iron-struck glowing blue of the tropics. There were some red ruffled streaks of white cloud towards the west. Here in ancient colonial poverty, unesteemed, I felt at home unto myself. There was no escaping the consequences of having left Europe. In Europe there'd been no escaping the consequences of having lived all of my life as I had, lived it in an all pervasive atmosphere of darkness, of candlelights of intelligence and studied effort showing an array of footsteps ahead. But none showed a clear individual purpose in my existence. There was never an illuminated belief in my mind. Never an illumination of past and future. Always the taste and ethos of living in absolute, benighted times. While others were as gloriously active and purposeful as lions in the warmth of the hunt. I could feel their bustle all around me, feel the primordial darkness and anger in their minds.

I described the world in terms common to those whom I was about, but I could never believe in those terms. Those who did seemed evangelised, socially and intellectually evangelised, mesmerised. There were common terms of class, social, economic, educational, accent, occupational, intellectual, racial, sexual, religious distinctions. These, the primary colours of society. An intuited creed of agenda and its vocabulary. A settled and fortified ethos to nudge and guide and gently rein perceptions and goals by economic and social rewards and honours. And its basic sinister side, as active and horrifying as its basic paranoia. As if society were a regiment of efforts and ideals harnessed for a purpose not germane to it. But it marched along, merrily or even grimly, without asking why against the strengths and power of the many buglers.

I needed candles of narcotics or alcohol to illuminate a private, tiny portion of the noonday darkness. Then I was wide awake to my place in the world, and nervously alerted to it, watchful of it. This, my primary response to sentient existence. The immensity of uncoopted, unevangelised, free energy in me, without a massive goal to channel it, needed sedation, of narcotics or alcohol. Happiness I knew, like everyone else, intense happiness, and as brief as a lightning flash in the night's sky, yes, and the rest was plod and trudge to a purpose I could not believe nor understand nor fathom. I came, privately, to terms of acceptance and surrender to my own mistakes, my own stupidities. The slow eating of my pride and the crumbling of my self.

This inner tragedy, this inner denouement, has a unique punishment; it is already finished, it is already completed, in the act of acknowledgement of the wasted years, and the continuing tragedy that these years are unredeemable to use or life, consciously dead and unredeemable in one's consciousness, as if one's consciousness were a well-filled graveyard of wasted life, useless experience. And there it was said to myself; my existence was a well-filled graveyard of wasted effort, of lost endeavours and unharvestable life.

And here beside me in this young woman there was something alive and luminous, distinct from the determined beauty of her face and manner, a state I only thought I could remember at one time in myself. Something I had lost and forgotten in myself through the years I could just see again in her. And it was as if she were allowing me to see this.

'One hundred and forty years ago, about, I used to get drunk with a Gringo called Harry Melville,' I said, but already Lia's eyes had snapped out of their stare. Her head and body moved forward in a gasp, but her eyes swivelled sideways to me and I could feel the heat of their affection. She rocked back and, in her sparkling new manner, turned to face me.

'Even you aren't that old,' she said, in a voice that was beginning to brim with happiness.

'Harry said poverty was worse than old age. It was old age. We were young when he said that. Now I'm old and broke, Lia.'

'But you're not poor,' she said, amazed, 'Sylvia wants another lesson, and Yara and Norma, and Yusmely who already knows all of 'Hey Jude' off by heart but only understands a few of the words, and Solange and Tereza. You could make sixty dollars today. Megabucks. Put them all together and make it in one hour!' Her delight was intense.

'You arranged this? You have this already arranged?'

'Of course,' she said, as if I would have found it amiss if she hadn't; and she was glad to prove she was ever so ready to be good; a pre-obedient little girl. It's not a trait I can condemn.

'Why did you take your bag from my room, our room?'

'You know you sleep with your arms folded,' she said,

'Just like a Buddha. It's very nice to watch you sleeping. I was sad to leave you.'

'Me too.'

'I can fix the lesson for six o'clock, in the Central Bar. I can book a room for an hour.'

'All right.' And I thought that would be good. Then I could get seriously drunk, and in the fast companionship of alcohol bravely examine myself and my situation. Just for one last time.

She settled against me and began to make herself comfortable. She said Maria had made her eat so much pasta, and special sauce — and did I get my special milk for breakfast? — and it's a sort of home-made narcotic, Maria's special sauce, an onion of garlic, not just a clove, boiled in its skin and mixed with crumbled garlic; and she had felt deeply contented and wandered unsteadily about the house, looked into the room, felt guilty that I had gone to bed without food, and had taken her bag away in repentance. Maria sent her to another room to sleep, and then had come to sit with her, and began an old Italian remedy. She whispered into her ear, but too softly to be heard. She complained, but Maria soothed her and continued her whisperings. Sleepiness was delicious, heavy and gentle in its coming, and finally Maria's whispering became as soothing as a lullaby, and she fell asleep, content and happy. She awoke full of spirit and energy and happiness. Radiant as Yara making up lies to tell and astonish, as I would learn. She came to see me but I was still sleeping like a Buddha. Maria said the new Irishman was a strange man, and would be very good or very bad for such a young woman. She told Maria we felt we had known each other a million years, and Maria said she'd give me special milk at breakfast, and keep the two of us on a special diet until a natural life returned to us.

Her face turned up to me like a child's and she asked if I knew what that meant.

No.

No, and Maria would not tell her.

'She knows I'm an undead corpse,' I said. And Lia jerked upright, her eyelids opening full and all the long-dead tiredness disappearing from her shocked eyes.

'Unborn babies, undead corpses. Something like that, Lia.'

She looked long at me, as if I were mad, and incredibly, she moved slightly, almost reluctantly, made herself more comfortable, closed her eyes and began to go to sleep again.

'Hey! You want to go to Maria's?'

'No,' she said, without opening her eyes, 'She'll only make me eat more pasta and garlic.'

'Walkies walkies, then?'

She mumbled and began to pull herself into wakefulness.

That numbing look of tiredness, of suppressed tiredness, was again all about her eyes.

She took my hand and we walked across the Square and out onto the main avenue. She looked at odd things in the shop windows, often put her fist to her mouth and mumbled odd things, but never loitered long. Opposite the theatre she stopped and asked me to read the incised latin numerals. MDCCLXXIV. This theatre was opened in 1774. Good God. A small Brazilian city, and its theatre was in operation since 1774.

Is this like the O'Leary story? I asked her. And she fell away laughing and pulled me along.

'Culture is important,' she said, 'you know that. It's important to us.'

And then, half to me and half to the fist again in her mouth as she inspected a window display, 'The stories of other people's lives.'

That was the first time I heard even an echo of bitterness in her voice.

But also it was groggy. There was something groggy, intoxicated, altered, in her. I asked her again if she wanted to sleep. She stamped and said 'No!' Then smiled and said 'Look, I'll show you a famous house.'

This was the city residence of a woman who had twenty children, and like all Brazilian women, almost, strove to give them unique and distinguished names. So she called them one, two, three, etc. But not in Portuguese, in French. and Diezhuit had been elected to the National Congress. She shrugged — and it was amazing, but she shrugged identically to my manner of shrugging my shoulders — and said, dismissively, it was nothing. Did I know that in Brazil they had the Lapinha Cavern. And that was ten million years old?

'Lia!'

I tightened my grip on her hand, pulled on her, turned her, and led her by the hand back towards the centre. She stumbled, but made no manner of complaint. What she had said was true. On the voyage to this place I had read it all and more in a book of Brazilian history.

On the corner of the main Square I stopped at a café and ordered two coffees. I put two spoonfuls of sugar into Lia's. Without tasting the coffee she reached and slowly began putting spoonful after spoonful more into her coffee. After three I stopped her. She sipped the coffee, grimaced, and spat it out. Then she laughed. But despite all the worn tiredness in her eyes, there was a flickering request for forgiveness, as if I might hurt her. I was about to order another coffee when her hand tightened and shook in mine.

'You look older than me,' I said.

She nodded her head and her eyes opened wider than a child's. 'I know,' she said, and made an act of a woman pretending to be a little girl, 'and I'm more mature, too. So there.' And immediately her eyes intensified and she searched my face for signs of hurt. Then her hand pulled on mine and we went back to Maria's. But her hand never eased its initial, frightened grip. She bent her arm and slowed me somewhat as we approached the door.

Maria, alerted by my manner and my first shouted question as to why she gave home-made poisons to people, was as conciliatory and concerned as if Lia were an innocent but wayward child. She was hugged, briefly, and her face examined, briefly, then passed all right and sent to wash and told to come thereafter to the dining room.

'Was she with Sylvia?' Maria asked.

'Yes.'

'It's nothing very strong,' she said, but showed little direct interest in explaining. She pulled out a chair for me at the table. All the town knew Sylvia gave her girls tranquillisers, she said, and it wouldn't matter if the girls were properly fed and properly rested; securely rested. That was why she had been insisting on the pasta and the garlic, now that Lia was safely staying here. The pasta and the special sauce didn't alter the mind, the mentality; it just resettled it back to its normal place during sleep. She only wanted Lia to sleep, and not to worry. And when Lia came back I should immediately ask her about Sylvia.

When she came back she looked re-energised and in full possession of herself, sat opposite me, drank a long swig from her water glass, and smiled at me. When I asked why she'd gone back to Sylvia she looked affronted, and said softly it was just security, she wanted some security; and did I understand? and her voice curtly clipped the last words. I nodded, anxious to reassure her, and said yes, of course. Then Maria came and placed bowls overflowing with pasta in front of each of us. I looked at Lia. She looked like she was falling back into grogginess and was on the verge of laughing in sympathy for me. I didn't want the food, but I had no problem eating it. I finished before Lia, and she continued eating contentedly and with solid appetite. Maria was silent. I sipped water and sat back. Lia was content, almost formally content, and Maria was silently eating. And the moments stretched out softly and comfortably. The odd sounds of eating, and the quietening sound of the city before siesta. Perturbable moments, but all of ease and peace. A fork scraped against a plate. Lia, Maria, and I sat in domestic familiarity. It was artificially incongruous, and it felt historic. I too was heavy with sleep.

And trust. I who had lost all trust, even in myself, above all doubted and subverted myself, felt the warmth of trust between us. Trust is not a commonplace. I had watched my own die. I had once achieved success, in my own life on my own terms. However petty, trite, or unimportant to others it was all to me; it was the fulfilment of a lifelong dream. Not just to be a published writer, but by that to have my legitimacy as a human being, and the legitimacy of my efforts, acknowledged and vindicated. This is not a commonplace; and it is, with primeval vagueness, the inner landscape and climate of every writer.

It was all to me. My innermost identity was reflected out; and, like the strangest waif, received acceptance. I found, found within myself, my own stature; found my own confidence, love and trust.

And then I watched in amazed disbelief as this edifice of self was demolished, by strokes of commission and omission, and watched my life, its very foundations, turned into a vandalised ruin. All the while I could not believe that this was happening to me. Without even a sheen of daydreaming, or the hypnotised focusing of intent that protects human sanity during the violence of physical attack, I watched in slow motion the efforts of my life turned to rubble. I was as amazed as any other victim that this was, unbelievably and without logic, justice, reason, happening to me. And like all victims I unthinkingly expected aid and succour. Literally I starved, went hungry, was cold, shivered from lack of heat, and waited like a beaten animal on a mountainside. Waited for the moon itself to pity me, answer the cries that I daren't make out loud. My mind broke down, under the weight of its own disbelief. All of the efforts of all the most pertinent years of my life turned to dust and ruin about me. How could I say this in other than the vocabulary and tone of a victim? But I did not want to tell it to Lia in that manner. And I had to tell her that the dust and the ruins I was talking about were me, not external to me, but me, and my new inner landscape and climate. As plaintive as that. And that the mental act of forgiveness is a sham. I had first to find my own human-ness again, before I could accept another's for being as weak, selfish, and conceited, and as vulnerable as my own. And as valid, for whatever human validity is worth.

Tired Lia and silent Maria were still about their food, silent in their sleepy, ebbing thoughts.

At that moment Lia sat back, sated. A moment later Maria put her fork to the side, sipped gladly from her water glass, and relaxed. She placed her elbows on the table. Still, no one spoke; there appeared to be no need for it.

My thoughts were away somewhere when Maria asked: 'Have you a family in Europe?'

'No.'

'No wife? No girlfriend?'

'No.'

Lia began to collect the plates. She looked embarrassed. Maria said she'd clear away the table. Then she and Lia exchanged some sharp and friendly elements of territoriality about this task, but Maria insisted, and sent us away to our siesta. ·

In our room Lia threw her bag over the bed towards the window.

And where it landed I noticed, standing in pristine delight, the bottle of noble whiskey she'd bought for me the previous evening. Then she pressed off her shoes, and immediately went to lie down dressed on the bed. I felt the same, and fully clothed in trousers and teeshirt lay down beside her. We wanted to hug and be hugged, but also we were relentlessly tired and wanted to lie this way and that, and finally we curled up privately beside each other. Sleep was anxious to come and we were anxious to take it. An imperative conditioning of childhood impeded my snug progress towards sleep and I slipped my arms out of my teeshirt and wore it as a cover rather than an article of clothing. I chuffed humorously to myself at this good little boy's ever obedient response. Then there was another thought; a thought of adult selfishness: that my arms were safely away from Lia's reach, should she have another nightmare in her siesta.

Sleep was no disappointment. From the satisfaction of heavy exhaustion, my mind, willowy, came to dip into beautiful dreams; of Lia sitting at home in some European sitting room, at night, of an unlaced dressed window showing a gently dark night and snowflakes falling, of Lia softly padding across the room and upstairs to check on them for a moment, of a long, long time of her absence, of her return, the quiet happiness on her face a parable of beauty. Then she came to me and gave me the love of her presence; and we sat, silent, and watched the midnight sky. It was happiness.

There was a whirlwind outside the window. It came as if from another dream. Broken images of people, of crowds in

Europe. The torn-clothed shuffle of the poor, the homeless, the bowed heads of Europe's teeming underclasses, as if from another century, teeming ranks of the emotionally, and the mentally, broken, the dishevelled, the hopeless, and the fierce glare of the intellectually-fired burning in humiliated wait for night shelters, for soup kitchens, to open. Centuries of progress, of development, of political thought, led to night shelters and soup kitchens, and the fear of insecurity as a factor of production. A private, cowled anxiety, not pride, was now the common aspect of the populace. Their faces, the recent change in the physiognomy, the brutalised lines of the charitably fed, the remnant ugliness of the faces, the fresh vulgarity, of all manners, gestures, features, of the left behind, those living daily in the inner gulags of Europe's re-emergent, recast cities with their concrete filing-cabinet highrises and other estates of slums of penitentiary layout, aspect, atmosphere. The new ugliness on the faces is medievally staggering. It is not just aesthetic ugliness, it is an anti-human ugliness. An acidity of ugliness, as if it showed a skulking, scowling mentality rabidly eager for the vengeance of gross, or petty, criminality. All nurtured in dole-penal areas of shabbiness, dankness, and rising hopelessness. Perhaps there will be no outcome, no harvest, no consequences from this flooding tide of hopelessness, from all these lives of nonexistence, of so many alive only to humiliation and deprivation, there in a Europe of tabloid TV and bestselling books most haughtily unaware that human life and culture and literature are not games of trivial pursuit, nor of adventure stories and fairy tales told for adults.

I was glad to withdraw again behind my window, to the dreamed warmth of family life, and have these rising masses disappear, disappear if only from the immediate neighbourhood of my frightened consciousness.

In my dream Lia was reading. There were opened books all around her, on the floor, on the sofa, on her lap. I went to lounge on the carpet near the fire, and picked up an interesting book lying there. On the coffee table there were just-baked scones steaming as they absorbed wedges of butter, and tea in a porcelain teapot was drawing its most secret flavours towards fulfilment. It was superb happiness. I groaned, in want, in regret, in pining for a life I'd never known except in dreams in my sleep.

The dream dissolved to a vaporous consciousness of itself. I clawed it back, to lodge it in memory as if it were an experience. Its presence and atmosphere left, and I, tired and in a slump of spirit, sighed and turned to inert and mindless, deep sleep.

There was sweet, recuperative oblivion for a while. All the well-fed rest of a tropical siesta. A dim, almost normal consciousness came. Lia and I were moving each the other way and bumping into each other. Again and again I gave way. Again and again she pulled me back by the shoulder. No matter how I settled next to her she was still discontented. I tried to accommodate her and always failed. I put my arms about her body and hugged her close. Her discontent eased, and immediately I slipped back into sleep. I surfaced into a clear but altered consciousness. Her body was limpid to mine and pressing with ultimate force. She sensed my wakefulness and eased her pressure. Her head rose and she kissed at my throat. I left her doing this and haphazardly discarded my clothes. Then my hands set to feeling her body. It was like an animal smelling, then felling, food on the hoof. I could smell the burned craving of her mouth, of her body.

I stripped her, slapping at any waywardness of co-operation that mis-matched mine. She was overwrought and snatching at breath. I spread her, felt that she was already wet, and mounted her. She placed her arms housewifely about my neck and laid her mouth limp open for my succour though I rode her with determined, steady thrusts. I took her knees over my shoulder and let her buck as she reached orgasm, but slapped her firmly when she threatened to lag on me. With a headstrong sense I dumbly refused to accept any errant nonsense from her body as I rode and husbanded it with a blind, determined fastness and loyalty. I dominated and husbanded her body steadily, and when she began to buck uncontrollably I gave my lust its heads and shook her with great lengthy strides to a heaved and seeded conclusion. She was all about me, arms and legs and her mouth pacifying my throat. It was sumptuous and warm and replete and sated. I had an immense tenderness for her and kissed and soothed her and rode her lightly as her body urged. Then we were both fully in normal consciousness, anxious for each other's concerns.

I was changed. There was a long-striding, haughty confidence in my attitude. The world was very manageable, and I was very strong. And so was Lia. We spoke to each other in some improvised language of bodies, intermingled breath, and mumbling words that always ended in shared smiles for each other's joy. I was glad for each grain of her, glad to take all the trust and responsibility she gave me, glad to give to her all the trust and responsibility she craved to take.

Later we went to shower. And washed and sparkling clean we went down to sip coffee and drink water with Maria. Strangely, I felt left-out and redundant in the animated but plain conversation. It didn't matter. The water was chilled and delicious to each sip of the coffee; and while I was musing about my altered state of mind, Maria, who had been speaking to me without my awareness, gave up trying to make me hear and went ahead to do what she had proposed. She snipped a small piece of lemon rind and slipped it gently into my coffee. This had something to do with the caffeine, she said, and once was the only way coffee was drunk in Italy. Or in that ancient part of ancient Italy from whence she had come, as a girl bride, in a postal marriage, the stock-breeding callousness of it, because she had been sold, sold like all the others, sold by the circumstances and prohibitions and traditions and ....

I was rising and making towards the door and Lia was laughing. Maria went silent, and the eternal gracious smile of an old lady flickered about her face. Maternally she told me to first drink my coffee, then go, and make money.

Hence, gunless, Lia and I went up to the rapidly darkening street towards the Central Bar. The sun moved across the sky with great speed and benevolence. The sky was a lake of colours. Ruffles of fire-red streaks glowed through ink-black clouds and illuminated the last of the day. And then it was suddenly fully fledged night. There was a perceptible drop in temperature. So much mystery and magic in the world. It was so good to be in life, to be an active participant in life.

The man who once was Irish, from Cork, was awake in his lair. We saluted him, got no answer but a quizzical examination of me, and walked on. Lia quietly and insistently urged me to speak English to him, to prove he wasn't Irish, but Portuguese. I had no doubts and tried to assure her. There was so much background I had to tell her. So many things whose intimacy I would not have told her before, but to which she now had a natural right. I promised her; but first we needed to make this money.

The taste of lemon rind and coffee was still so unusually pleasant in my mouth that I forwent the beer while Lia hustled my clients, agreed the price, and collected the cash. The bar wanted to charge the group-sex rate for the room, and Lia negotiated a more modest price. It was only for an hour and no towels or bedding would be disturbed. The bar itself was too noisy and distracting, and the central Square now too chilly.

Lia told me the room was the famous room. Nailed to the wall over the bed and under a painting of the Virgin Mary suckling her child, was a blue plaque. It was of that colour, that battleship grey, Confederate grey, that so many sailors call sea blue. And the wood was the soft skinned utility wood always found aboard ships. On it, in plain Latin letters quite neatly grooved by a carpenter's punch, was the fable of O'Leary and his one hundred and forty-seven women. It started in Latin, went to sailor's French and Portuguese, changed to English in its rush to exaggerate, then ended again with hang-overish, humble Latin. It was nailed solidly to the wall and may have been there for all of forty years. There was some emerging, antique grace to it. And the girls loved it and revelled in it as a direct communiqué from another long dead generation. Their tastes, their habits, their circumstances, had only an outward show of change from O'Leary's, from the unknown sailor who had whiled away his seatime creating this memorial to a fable. We were all on the same farm, just passing through the time of our fate, and trying to beguile and venerate ourselves as pleasantly as we might.

I was glad to start the lesson. Yusmely smiled, all her

tropical charm flowing out of the great batting of her eyelids. But she would not say a word. I coaxed. And Yara, as primly as a little schoolgirl, asked me to speak up please. Once my petting attention was distracted from Yusmely, and I focused on Yara, I thought I actually saw a trail of jealousy being guiltily hidden in her eyes and features. But it went from one to the other, even, dear Jesus, to acquisitive Sylvia.

Having long lost any regard for myself I did not mind. I began to sing 'Hey Jude!' and found myself with an uncontrollable riot of hysterically laughing women. Even Lia was laughing, though I thought she also looked proud. And thus, out of pity for me, Yusmely spoke the first line of the song. And how appropriate it was and they all laughed again. But slowly we began to make it better. It was so easy, so gentle, so pleasant, an occupation. I had never imagined it could be so. They were getting the words fluent and natural, and in a little pause, almost like a contented pause during a meal, Yara said they didn't have any girls for lesbians in the Central Bar. Those girls hung out at the Panorama Bar, where the man who once was Irish, from Cork, earned his miserable living as a car-minder. And that was probably why O'Leary had come here and not to the Panorama. It was amazing. Their simple gullibility. Despite the native brightness of their considerable intelligence they were willing, even anxious, to hear and believe the most outrageous tales. It was as if they found truth in them, not the everyday manufactured truth and lies of common speech, but unchanging human truths that reassured them of their rights and place in the world. There was no choice but to leave them follow the scents and echoes they took from each word and let them randomly chase all. It came near to bedlam, sometimes, and often from this bedlam came shafts of illumination that were rarely lexical. They played with the melody, and with the melody of each word and grew acquainted with the oddities of accent of pronunciation, with the quick and the pausing memories and echoes of association mixing into their private thoughts. And often they fumbled, they themselves fumbled over and about with the words, and when they did so they seemed to understand more, to see more deeply into the vistas of humanity beyond the labelling words. They became more receptive, more instinctively aware of the fragility of meaning in each word, and the wavering mirage of meaning in all language.

Before Lia, unceremoniously, said it was time, the hour was finished.

Then she began her quick and direct negotiations for another class. I had only myself to collect before leaving the room. And since the negotiations were hinging on Lia insisting on a price increase, I left the room and made for the bar. Sylvia also broke away from the group. In the hallway she said it was very important for the girls to learn English. The only seamen left, the best customers, were Dutch and Filipino and Greek and Korean, and so it was quite essential that the girls speak rudimentary English. But nothing more. Just numbers and the common lies of affection and arousal and encouragement and satedness, the repertoire-words of American and English women during quick sexual activity. I said I was flattered, but had insufficient experience to do this.

'You are greedy,' she said, 'you know.'

'Shall I teach that word to your girls, Sylvia?' I asked, 'and let them explore what it means? In plain Portuguese? Would you like that?'

I could see the challenged neanderthal gluttony and slyness clear in her eyes. For a free plate of gruel on the bad days she held these trusting waifs hostage to their poverty and innocence. Nothing else. And got almost all they earned on the good days. Language was something less than a beautiful utility for the clarification and expression and maintenance of our humanity; it was a cheap adornment from which the girls would make themselves more employable and productive of hard cash.

But then a freak thought crossed my mind. It was directly connected to the deep confidence in myself Lia had engendered that afternoon.

'Work with me, Sylvia,' I said. 'Work with me and you'll get what you want. More. But don't insult me, ever, you fascist pig. Or I'll break your fucking neck.'

I turned to go.

'You want more money, don't you,' she said. I couldn't resist it. I turned to her. 'Read my lips, Sylvia. Read my fucking lips.'

The bar was almost empty. Most of the regulars, and the expected casuals, were somewhere else taking their evening meal. I had Maria's glorious food, and hers and Lia's company awaiting me, and so I settled for a chilled bottle of the glorious beer. There was no sense of having earned it; it was a simple, cleansing dessert to an ample pleasure. And the cigarette added *élan* to my inner atmosphere.

Lia arrived and stood next to me. We looked at each via the mirror. There were flicks of humour puckering about her eyes.

'I've got sixty dollars for you. Sixty US dollars,' she said in a whisper.

'Fifty-fifty?' I asked.

'One hundred — One hundred.'

'OK.'

'Tomorrow,' she said. 'There'll be more. Sylvia is paying for them, for all the girls.'

'Investing in her employees?'

'Only Maria would say something like that.'

'Bravo for Maria.'

She smiled, a bashful, wide-eyed smile. 'It was only yesterday morning. And you misunderstood so much. Maria would not let any girl use the house for business.'

The other girls were now coming into the bar and settling themselves about the tables. In the mirror I saw Yara approach me and waited for the expected grab on the buttocks. Instead she put a friendly hand on Lia's shoulder and said in English, tunefully: 'Then you begin to make it better?'

Lia smiled, Yara smiled. And a hand slipped and viciously pinched my right buttock.

'Haa!'

'Better ... better ... better,' crooned Yara, satisfied, and increased the breadth of her smile, tapped her fingers on

Lia's shoulder, and turned to slink across to Yusmely, the silent witness to it all.

Lia's smile was like that evening's setting sun. Then she told me she and Yara came from the same school. I thought she meant background, experience, but she said no, the same school; a very normal school she had once loved very much. She and Yara used to swap books, all kinds of books, and used to go to pray in the middle of the night so that they could read books under the candlelight of the chapel.

I asked for another beer and a shot of whiskey. I was afraid of what was coming.

'You understand?' she said. 'You are Irish and Catholic.'

Many moments passed, many moments. I was shaking my head. It is so impossible to escape being held to the Irish stereotype, the one inalterable, universal version of Irishness. And for this I blame not just my beloved and phlegmatic, sober English, but those Irish for whom there is most definitely just one possible, most holy, unalterable and universal, version of Irishness. As if there were any version of any nationality, of that relic of nineteenth-century sectarianism elevated to a state of established bigotry by another name; medieval theology in a continuation and extension of its wars for power, booty, and loot by other means. And the lambs born on the farms, the Lias and the Yaras, have not slightest inkling of the traditional husbandry of their thoughts, and by the very means that thereof they are taught to call their culture.

'Hmm?' she asked.

'I can't myself remember that, Lia.'

And she thought I was joking.

'But I'm only a Catholic sometimes now,' she said. 'And so is Yara.' She gave me one of her soft smiles, her eyes searching my face for clues, her smile so ready to alter, always altering, to take and give acceptance and never to release or weaken the bond between us. I took her hand in mine and softly squeezed. 'Don't tell me any more. I don't want to know any more.'

'Take another beer,' she said, 'and then let's go back to Maria's. I think I could sleep again.' Her voice had softened, as if she were telling me a confidence. 'Maria will be pleased if I tell her I want to sleep again.'

I paid attention to the look of her eyes. They weren't so haggardly tired as before, but there was a tiredness there, a tiredness old and unsuited to her age.

We took the beer and went to sit at a table. I noticed Yara. She tilted her head to one side in apology, thinking she had caused a disagreement. I nodded, just to mislead her.

The difference between social life in Latin America and in Europe or North America is inexpressibly immense. The South Americans live by life alone. They are the most racially mixed people the world has ever known. And in their endless and visible and mostly violent pushing and shoving for place and position they have never known security of life or property. Thieves hunt in packs in the streets; almost all avenues of advancement are blocked and reserved by families of wealth. And between these extremes people rise and fall in the struggle for life like the crests and troughs of a violently stormy sea. And for causes as simple in expression and as complex in origin.

It is the world's richest, least populated continent, and it has never known regulation, social peace, security. It is a continent that has never, beneath the level of its elites, known any economic order other than free-market capitalism. All elites, everywhere, for me, are the inscrutable camp administrators of society, ceaselessly making up rules and theories — for other people — as they go along with their privileged, unrationed, monied lives.

In all their magnificent and uncountable colours and

species, the birds of this continent of refuge pluck the seeds
of its multitudinous fruits, and its fruits, untended, grow in
abundance everywhere. Its climate is magnificence. And the
social ambience is everywhere of acceptance and tolerance
of the sadness and harshness of life; and a keen and hungry
appreciation of all the parallel joys and pleasures forever
ripe and succulent, and anxious to be plucked, *now*. And
savoured, *now*.

South Americans like foreigners and quite naturally treat
them as pleasant provincials; as still living folklore that
provides some insight into ancient countries and attitudes;
some anecdotal, private understanding, some hunch, into
the mysterious ways and byways of genetics' inscrutable,
extra-dimensional, immutable laws of biological
continuation and, alas, mutation.

Most Brazilians don't believe that human nature, the
nature of any animal, can change at all. And by human
nature they mean sexuality and its rituals. Life evolves
about sexuality; sexuality is the untamperably active,
volcanic core of life, and they are astonished that elsewhere
it is considered otherwise. Or deemed a facet of the mind,
and as subject to encompassing, mental control as
toothache. This cheapjack European, this homeopathic
European philosophy — from the continent that cursed the
entire globe with its mass slaughterers, its endless wars to
end war, its Hitlers, its Stalins, the bloody-handed
philosophies of Communism, Fascism, Capitalism. It is a
source of despair to them. And then to be preached to and
admonished by people whose continent's history is a
cesspool of inhumanity, and whose inhabitants are, *a
fortiori*, the descendants of those who carried out the
butcheries, or the odd and reduced progeny of the victims.
Especially when they are treated to admonitions on their
unconsciously relaxed sexual activities, and admonished for

their economic backwardness by a continent that brutalised
and exploited them for three centuries.

Simply, they treat their sexuality with a bemusement
exactly akin to that normally enjoyed by a European
housepet. And it is more or less as freely indulged, knowing
that it must feed, must take natural nourishment upon the
hoof, if it is not to become inexplicably warped in itself, and
hence go self-chained into insanity. We acknowledge not
just the animal, but also the beast in our human nature. And
from the mind and intellect we expect all it can deliver:
consolation, not salvation. There is a pervasive ethos here
that human life is a sad joke, that we all live tethered on the
same farm of humanity, that we are of a species that farms
itself. And there is considerable kindness, considerable
generosity of spirit, a nobility, in understanding the
inevitability of our suffering and our useless doom, servant
to our beast. The animal is the need to feed and shelter the
body, the beast is the panic to do so that turns our minds to
all their imbecilities, cruelties, perversions.

I say this, of course, not as a sociologist, nor professional
traveller, but as one who had the essence of his life wilfully
destroyed, had his biological life almost destroyed, by the
random, dumb cruelty direct from the stock that produces
Europe's camp guards, the well- and the normally-bred, the
well- and the normally-cultured — cultivated — endless
stock of those who administer, adjudicate, regulate, and
enforce the running of society. In all their rushing, pushy,
shoving arrogance; the ironically literal classless
apparatchiks who service state power, any state's power.

How proud, how gloriously proud I was, to attend at the Mansion House of the capital city of a west European nation, to shake the Lord Mayor's hand, and to receive an award called the Brendan Behan Memorial Fellowship. This was acceptance, this was validation, indeed. This led directly, within months, and with my numbed compliance, to the undoing and the destruction of all I had worked all my life to achieve. Nothing much, but all to me. It led further. It led to my poverty. It led to standing by a village crossroads, just one more man of a number in the unformed crowd waiting for the police car to arrive, waiting to sign our names for entitlement to the minimum state aid for the unemployed. That morning it led, not comically at all, to the flared nostrils and bared teeth of the angry cop telling me I wasn't Irish, to get to fuck out of his sight, that he would deal with me, that he would fix me, that he would see to me. These are not threats of compassion.

And so, under the auspices of the Brendan Behan Memorial Fellowship I lived off the dole of other unemployed men, which is dole indeed, Brendan. This is true. All of the many promises of the award were pre-broken. But I traded all that I had, which was not poverty, not disenfranchisement, was very little but considerably more than nothing, for those empty words. Even to the last, to the saying of goodbyes, to making my farewells, holding close to me for precious moments those friends who cried because I was taking my leave of them. And less than four months later I was nervously and mentally broken, and shied away from letting them see me on the streets. My trust, my life, exchanged for pre-broken promises. What others had to gain from this perplexes me to this day, and has perplexed more than one psychologist. I will never know. But the documents are there, the witnesses exist. Ireland, Eire, Anno Domini 1983, 1984.

Please note the century.

All of this, all of all the torn, bloodied, dismembered details of this bedlam of lies and deceits running through my mind, again and again, endlessly daily, nightly, for years, inextricably woven into contradictory beliefs of muddled hopes, acts, concerns, the knots and revulsions that had twisted and perverted my life and my mind for aeons. It seemed. Now it slipped and fell, unexpectedly, into the past. Its confining, lethal grip on my mind had loosened.

Lia was sitting quietly in her own thoughts beside me, and I felt I was in the presence of magic, and magically came the first genuine feeling I had felt in years. It came without shock, a beacon that flickered, then held fast; it had the power to control my body and a rush of dread arrived in my stomach. I had no response to it, and it was telling me now the worst that it could tell me: that I knew I was a liar, a faker, a trickster. That this was true. That all was true. That I had survived the swamp of lies and deceit and the suffocation of my life. I had lived through it. I had come, just now, out of a long illness from a bad wound, and the first definable touch of my return to normality was the taste of my own deceit. And the taste of deceit everywhere.

I had spent hours in public health, public welfare, psychiatric hospitals, in those whitewashed cubicles, pouring out my life's story, sober, or drugged or under hypnosis, and all that came out contained no solution, no resolution, to itself. Now it was suddenly defined and whole and complete and in the past, foreclosed, dead, of no living matter. A learning experience or a teaching environment it didn't matter; it no longer coralled my life. I was free of it. And my first taste was of deceit, deceit that was already up and running.

Yara sat next to Lia and whispered something. Lia shook

her head and looked surprised and looked at me.

No one within twelve thousand miles knew anything true about me, but I was instinctively and cleverly adapting myself to all of their assumptions; as cleverly as only instinct can. I was actively allowing their assumptions to turn into my lies; into constraints, and their definition of me. Without great care I would recreate here all the catastrophic foundations of my old life in Europe. I could not, I must not, expect *myself* to be its old self in the New World, unless I was willing to replicate my mistakes all over again.

'We're not talking about you,' Lia said with such radiant credibility that I had to think twice before I could make myself definitely believe that they were, absolutely and undoubtedly, talking about me. But it was youthfully quaint of them to expect me to believe them, and in enchantment for their innocence I smiled back my reassurance with exactly their open measure of hypocrisy. It couldn't hold. My smile turned into reluctant laughter. Immediately both Lia and Yara blushed and turned to cuddle each other in laughter.

'Sylvia says you carry a gun,' Yara whispered. 'And you really want to take over as our manager.'

'Manager?'

'That's Sylvia,' Lia stood up. 'She means pimp.'

Yara's face altered. She looked just what she was, little more than a child, seventeen, eighteen, and brutally reminded of the terrifying predicament of her life.

'She's only Sylvia,' Yara said.

And with the outstanding verbal and social skills that young women friends employ when having a disagreement, Lia and Yara commenced and concluded a quarrel about this that left neither one offended. It ended when Lia said: 'He loves me, that's all. He's a gentleman.

And tell Sylvia there's no more English lessons.'

Then she embraced Yara with a quick hug, turned to look back at Sylvia, for a fraction of a second, took my hand and led me out.

'I'm not a gentleman,' I said as soon as we turned into the street. She was too preoccupied with her own agitation to pay attention. But she had said nothing about the gun. She who remembered all and omitted nothing had said nothing about the gun. So it seemed she was deeply afraid of Sylvia; brave, even brazen, even smiling, to her face, and she was all the while very afraid of her. Very afraid. And I felt very protective of such gallantry.

Passing by the telephone exchange, and wanting to distract her agitation I spoke to the man who once was Irish. In the only Irish words I know I asked him his name. He replied in English, in a coarse, vulgarity of manner. And although I could plainly recognise a Cork accent, his accent dipped heavily into the ungainly, both plaintive and smug accent of the English tabloid classses; that grating accent of patronising soap-operas, of 'cor's, innit's, no wat ah mean loike mate', the squaddy English of the unread-classes. The only words said with a distinctive Cork accent were 'tourist' and 'satyriasis' and 'shame'.

Lia was astonished, and as anxious as a cat to understand the exchange. But I didn't understand satyriasis. I smiled and asked him what it meant. All became clear. Again in mock tabloid Englishness he replied: 'Ain't got much bleedin education, ave we, den.'

He looked astonished when I instantly laughed, coughed with laughter at him.

'I am right,' Lia said, amazed that she was. 'He doesn't speak English.'

Oh, all the petty maggots of the mind, in the muck of childhood indoctrination, all the tribal parochialisms and nationalisms that lead to such worn-out, shabby spite in an adult human brain. His petty spite was visibly dribbling from the mentality, the mesh, of his mind, and dribbled about his sneering, curled lips in sprays and spittles. Whatever the sounds, it was the language of a dumb beast. A dumb, unhoused beast.

'But what language is it?' Lia asked, transfixed.

'It's the language of a dumb beast,' I said out loud.

I was backing away and pulling her by the hand with me. The dog was growling and anxious to attack; and its master much less responsible than anyone with a knife or a gun, though his instrument was much more savage. I wished I had Maria's gun.

'He's a sick beast,' I said. Immediately the man moved, tried to move, tried to disentangle the chain holding back the beast.

'I'll blow its fucking head off, Limey, and yours too.'

He looked shocked. He pulled the dog back close and hugged it to him. Lia was silent as I stepped back and turned away. Just at the corner the man who once was Irish, from Cork, shouted in his entire native accent: 'Ya fuckin' Yank ya.'

'I called him "Limey",' I said, 'so he'd believe me. Can you understand that? To insult a bigot under the rubric and the assumption of two conflicting bigotries?'

She eased a little and smiled, but her eyes were mystified. She mistook her lack of this world's historical, mental pollution, of experience, for some lack of intelligence or education in herself. She shook her head, like an immigrant lost in a new world.

'I told you I never liked him,' she said.

But we had Maria to unlock the door and welcome us, and bolt and bar the door behind us, like a poet, from all the foulness without.

Maria had extended her menu. There was the compulsory
pasta, but it was followed by fresh pirarucu fish, huge
steaming fillets of it soaked in some homeopathic sauce. I
assumed it was such, but ate it with relish anyway. Lia ate
with a swift appetite and talked about the man from Cork.
Maria remembered when he had first come. He was
impressive, and many people felt esteemed to be his
acquaintances. He never expected less and behaved like an
oracle. That was when Maria decided he was sick, there, in
the head. This was before people began to suspect there
were hidden calculations in his friendship. At first they
could only see some foreign vanity that was unbecoming to
such a gentleman. Then gossip crossed some of his lies and
opinion began to double-check him, and soon he was ill
regarded and no longer treated as a serious man. After
some time this finally came to his notice and he resented it
and many times upbraided many people for it. Finally he
began to disregard people, to disdain them for not taking
him at the correct measure of his own estimation. He
became a burden to the shipping agency he worked for, was
dismissed, set up a rival firm and went bankrupt; imperial,
and wagering on miracles to save him, to the bitter end.
And lost all.

   Then he broke his long avowed hatred of alcohol and
began to drink with the forest Indians whenever they were
in town. They were forever courteous and respectful of all
people — when in the city — and smilingly listened to his
endless advice and admonitions, although most couldn't
understand Portuguese. Next he was assistant manager at
the Panorama of Lesbians — they need a lot of men there
because the women and girls fight, physically fight, a lot
with each other — next he was safeguarding the cars of the
business women who came daily to visit their business
girls. And now no one noticed him at all. They would next

notice him when they had to shoot his dog, and bring the man who once was Irish, from Cork, outside the city limits to the cemetery, and silently bury his body.

It was a sad fate, that this was his only future.

I asked Maria what was to become of me. Lia had declared me professor, not a professor, but the professor of the Irish University of Cork. In the middle of the entire Central Bar. In front of everyone.

Lia was too quickly delighted and laughed over her food and nearly choked. But in the rushing warmth of our laughter Maria's smile lapsed for a moment and her eyes seriously, inquiringly, held mine. The shelter of her concern moved me. I could begin to believe that I was one of the lucky ones of this world. And I had Lia, who seemed to ask no more than that I should not stop her from loving me.

I believe in gratitude but, like sympathy, I have embarrassing trouble expressing it. I wanted something physical to do, to paint the room, or wash the windows or polish the floor, something to savage and devour the immensity of gratitude that had grown and flourished so rapidly within me.

I tried to say it. I said I had never felt so much thankfulness for friendship as I now was feeling; for their existence in my life, Lia and Maria.

Lia looked at Maria. They paused, fractionally paused; quizzicality a bridge between their alerted, communicating eyes. Quickly Lia said I needed sex again. And Maria quickly sighed for her, and commented on the burdens of being young and beautiful.

'And lusted after,' Lia added. Lust on lust on lust. By rambunctious old men romping up and down like wild stallions on their first day in pasture.

'And drinking,' said Maria.

'And not saving their money to take care of their adoring

lovers,' said Lia.

'And not changing their teeshirts in two days.' From Maria.

'If that were the least of it,' Lia.

'I spoke too quickly, too badly,' I said, embarrassed, and instinctively raised my hand and scratched my head, 'I'm sorry. It was too strange a thing to say.'

And their playful seriousness instantly erupted into hysterical laughter. I hadn't blushed since childhood, but I was blushing now.

'I think I'm not wanted here,' I said.

'Finish your dinner,' commanded Maria.

'And then go upstairs to your bottle.'

'OK. I will.'

I was feeling a sham, playful resentment, but I could easily have fallen into its own reality. They were trying to educate me to the sociability of our new relationship, and I would eagerly accept that. But there was no need to be so ham-fisted and flippant about it. They were succeeding to some extent because now I felt my emotions beginning to sulk. Lia's shoulder brushed solidly against mine. Her arm came about my shoulder and her other hand slipped down to my thigh. She brushed her face against the side of my face and licked me about the ear and I had to turn my head from the sensation and face her.

'I love you too,' she said. 'You know that. And you know that's true. You know that.'

Now I had to leave, had to go upstairs to my bottle. But there could be only one subject they wanted to talk about outside of my presence, I knew that then; they wanted to talk of the explanations and repairs they would have to make for the delicacies I had strained or blindly broken in the manner of my old world dealings with Sylvia and with the inconsequential man from Cork. This city was Lia's and

Maria's life, not just a social life, but their immediate and only universe, the shape and reflection of their concerns, the concerns of their immediate lives, here where they lived all their lives and acted and reacted to the weaves and strains of the communal life in their city. They had to make running repairs to the twists and distortions my casual, stranger's mistakes caused in their world.

'I understand,' I said, believing that I did. 'But in the Central Bar, Maria, Lia said she needed her sleep.'

They both laughed, like the most ancient grandmothers in the world.

'It is real,' said Lia, 'that sometimes I think the man loves me more than his whiskey.'

So I waved a dismissing hand at them both as I started upstairs to my whiskey.

'Germans often say things back to front,' I said as I went, and saw Lia's face dislike but forgive the remark.

There is celestial ichor in love, and it is replete when one is loved with such a diplomacy, the diplomacy that is the continuation of love by other means.

I was home. Sweet Jesus I was home. After all these years, coming to find my death, I had found my transient home in this world. Never, not in all the brief history of all of the time left for this universe, will any particle of me stop loving Lia. Never. I know that is true. I know that this is eternally true.

Upstairs I laid out my spare teeshirt and socks and underwear, turned off the light, and settled myself down on the floor to enjoy my bottle. Its cap cracked open with great satisfaction. So I was a failure in life. But there is more often more honour in that than in success. If there can be no credibility or objectiveness in the words of a failure, what can be learned from a failure's life honestly retold? It is not true that success must always be the embrace of the lowest common denominator. I had had success, and not from the lowest common denominator of public amusement. I received esteem and was rewarded for being a writer, a teller of tales; a craft I believe is the world's oldest and most satisfying profession. But the brief flicker of that once nourishing success died, was now dead in the old world whence I had come. Even now, under a new given name; and a new given life, I believe that the flicker of recognition of my craft and my commitment to it had been killed, its growing and strengthening life wilfully and maliciously extinguished. By those who do not understand that writing, too, holds a celestial ichor, the celestial ichor of all human community.

If she would only come now, and go to bed, and let me protect her. I would tell her stories now, of cats, of pill-poppers and peasants and princes and queens. And of liars and cheats.

I would never tell her any word of that coal black night in Yorkshire. In all the unspeakable and unspoken history of that land of Dickens it was a more apt time of Dickens than Dickensian times. Families and marriages and communities were being broken and dismembered and discarded by Stalinist economic decrees. The only people in committed opposition were cant raving Stalinists. But it made an ideological kind of sense to subsidise enforced idleness rather than to subsidise productive work. Mine-pit after mine-pit was being closed and rationalised out of existence in England and Wales. Thousands, thousands of the proudest of men were being broken one by individual one. Men whose backbone and families had won all the battles, including the then recent Falklands Malvinas War, were humiliated and reduced to the handouts of the modern laws for the subsistence of the poor.

It was economic sense to create and then subsidise

poverty. And humiliation, degradation, despair. Beggars and the homeless re-emerged from distant history and appeared on the streets of the great industrial cities of Britain. And the strikes and the pit closures went on and on and on. This crisis of a nation and the unravelling and destitution of hundreds of thousands of lives coincided with the petty remnant tragedy of my own life.

My memory shies away as powerfully as a frightened horse from any recollection or contemplation of the details. From an inner stature of faith in myself, and the courage and mental energy of that, I was reduced to beggary, in all its forms, minute by minute, day by day.

The Brendan Behan Memorial Fellowship Award promised two years at a US university, fees and board and lodging paid, plus a stipend of pocket money. This was more than ample for the wildest extent of my ambitions; it was a great, great deal to me. When I arrived only the university existed, absolutely innocent of the promises made in its name.

Innocent, unaware, disbelieving. Professor O'Aigisthos of the Irish Directory that controlled the Fellowship, and who had presented it to me, foisted me onto a fellow professor who kindly rejuggled his children around the bedrooms to create a spare bedroom for me. His wife gave me a welcome that a brother would envy. But I, having spent a lifetime recoiling from the mysteries of domesticity, found myself constricted and irked in the comfortable bosom of a normal, happy family, and I listened to their normal domestic concerns and loves, all the unimportant fights and quarrels and the quick and nasty disagreements of four children and their mother and father, day by day, at breakfast, lunch, dinner and supper, day by domestic day.

I was ungrateful. I asked Professor O'Aigisthos to provide me with the promised, private accommodation.

'I hear you,' he said.

Finally, when my over-stayed foisted presence was obviously becoming equally irksome to the family, I moved out. I found the best accommodation I could afford: a hovel. The man in the room next to me earned his food scavenging from the street garbage cans. This accommodation was a huge step up in the world for him. For him and for me avoiding the drop to sleeping on the sidewalk was a weekly nightmare; for both of us it took the energy of a gravity defying feat. Week by week.

Meantime Professor O'Aigisthos informed me that the terms of the Fellowship were 'not valid at this moment in time'. He meant today, tomorrow, and the rest of the century. I had to teach, the only possible source of income was to teach. There was no choice, no option. Even a ticket back home was out of the question.

The trauma must have been instant. I asked how dead children know to lie so tragically in men's arms? how grief stricken fathers know how to walk with a keenness of dramatic intent no actor can achieve; when art knows it is never more than life's poor cousin what value is art?

That, he said, was for the birds. You had to be positive, in this life, and take what you could get.

Not taking what I didn't want meant several hundred dollars of airfare that I didn't have.

Three days later I started, and then and thereafter, to quell my rebellious, my utterly frightened nervousness, with the aid of my fellow hoveller and a small bottle of illegal alcohol neatly poured into a water-beaker I entered the classroom; and made a tragic clown of myself.

I had no teaching qualifications. I wasn't even sure of the meaning of 'Creative Writing' other than as a fundamentalist study of the Bible, which I had never even read. I was here under duress, and if I had a work-permit I would gladly do anything else but this.

They just sat and looked at me, as if they had not been addressed. They were, the majority of the students, incredibly relaxed, and most were tolerant. One was nonchalantly eating a hamburger, and another kept smiling at me with teeth so white they'd shame a shark. Yet there was an absolute lack of hostility. During one pause, and I tried frantically to avoid pauses, I was casually asked to a pillow-party.

Perhaps writing is an active field of intuition, a nonsense, a fragmentation of character, organised daydreaming, a constant ambiguity and uncertainty of mind. Nevertheless, it is an intensely private act, and its inner processes cannot be mirrored out without changing those processes. Once self-consciousness intrudes, especially examination or classroom self-consciousness, all spontaneity is lost, the spirit stumbles, it becomes an act in the manner of theatre; but the suspension of disbelief is untenable, and the result is farce.

She finished her hamburger and popped open a coke. I swallowed the last of my alcohol.

Perhaps the process of writing, the germination of impulse, is governed by structured, developmental rules, immutable as in any organism, but knows no more of its science than an amoeba, cannot see itself without the act interfering with what it sees and thereby altering itself to another perception, and is utterly unable by itself to give an out-of-itself, objective, overall account of its own processes by its own processes.

Less than ten minutes of an entire hour had passed.

But I would not ask nor expect neither the rose nor the weed to teach creative gardening. And I would be obliged if no one attended class. All could be assured of full credit at the end of term. It was, anyway, a nonsense subject. Or they could go to administration and get their money back. Some did. One even wrote to the newspapers, explaining that he truly wanted to learn to write like Mickey Spillane, and I was unfit to teach him.

To the now outraged Chairman of the English Department I had to defend myself against this flattery.

The letters began to arrive, ordering me not to attend class as a student until I paid my fees, a mere eight thousand dollars. Then the weekly letters began to express formalised anger, and threatened legal penalties. Professor O'Aigisthos, when he was run to ground while being not sick, ill, or in meetings, assured me that just next week the cheque was coming. I was to hang on in there.

I was expected to hang-in like this for two full years, and to live for the academic year on a rate of pay that was one-quarter of the welfare rate. And on nothing for the remaining months.

I was living on water, potatoes, and raw bread. I managed, by exchanging one hunger for another, one want for another, to pay my weekly rent, managed my busfare for the hour long ride to and from the campus. All I had saved on the cheap airfare out was gone, all my savings were gone. I slept pillowless, sheetless, blanketless, on a bare mattress, using my streetcoat as covering. I sold books and clothing and knickknacks I had brought across the Atlantic with me. As often as once a month I sold a pint of blood at the local bloodbank, along with my hovelled friend who sold his blood when he felt the slightest flush.

Christmas came, two months after the first snow that lay four to five feet deep in a temperature that never rose above zero. Christmas went, on the northwestern seaboard of the United States. And in that beautiful, rich city I was more hungry, more hopeless, than an escaped prisoner on the Russian steppes.

And always the fear, the dampened-down panic that flushed into my stomach on awakening, flushed into my stomach constantly during sleep, of how I could possibly survive another day. Another day of nothingness, expectancy, officialdom's silence, and further nothingness. Everything was gone. The last friends and acquaintances had been squeezed of their last dime, or quarter or buck. I was shameless and hardened to asking; I was near to grasping. And the dumpsters and the trash cans yielded no Christmas bounty.

I know I often repeated myself endlessly in conversation, often returned twice to make twice sure that I had turned off the gas, or the electricity, or the water. But I didn't know that then. From the fragments of memories, in the luxury and peace I now enjoy, I can piece together the broken, denied memories in my mind.

Then my interest in conversation vanished. Any word would do for any other. Any grunt would do for any word. Day by day I waited for any word, any grunt. The silence from officialdom, and from the vanished O'Aigisthos, was as deep and impenetrable as the steppes. But not as genuine, and not as clean.

The pretence of teaching had long since stopped. Most of the students reluctantly realised that my poverty and my paralysed fear of offending officialdom, of giving just cause for utterly denying the Fellowship to me, which they had already done, was not European or artistic affectation, but genuine, and they dropped away.

And still my daily gloss over my shattered self-esteem continued with neurotic nicety. In this state of despair I was ever more than ready to instantly respond to any clink in officialdom's indifferent hostility. And to myself I denied that this was craven and abject surrender to fools and thieves whose interest in literature and the life of the mind was and always had been simulated, was faked, was totally derivative, aped, imitative, and all for the peasant's meal-ticket of an easy and an esteemed life, a life simulated and responding only to ego and greed, the pettiest of greed. That I did not have the courage to rebel and attack these peasants in any way is a cross I must still bear.

There was nothing more to sell. Of myself or anything else. The paltry money in my pocket was the last sum of money in my entire world, and could not feed last week's still present hunger.

There was nothing for anything that had to be paid that day; rent and food. There was nothing at all left. And I was ungracious in defeat. And yes, with the courage of a small bottle of illegal alcohol I forced and shoved and pushed my way past the university's president's secretary and showed and demonstrated the embossed promises of the Brendan Behan Memorial Fellowship under which I was supposed to be living. I was pushed out again. And within the hour the loudspeakers in the campus cafeteria were calling me back to the admissions office to collect the authorisation for my airticket back to Dublin for the following day. Not quite what I had expected, and I would anyway have preferred a less announced departure, but a day later I arrived back in Ireland.

But what was left for me there? I had bid it all farewell. Not just formally, but mentally and emotionally. I had bid it all goodbye.

Well there was shame. And there was incredulity, disbelief. What had I said or done wrong? I could understand that incredulity, that disbelief. I had lived it as a nightmare for four months. Many emigrants arrive back shattered and broke. Few arrive back mentally and emotionally disturbed, and penniless, from a guaranteed Fellowship in a United States university. Most have too much pride to do that. I had nothing but shame.

On borrowed money. I went to Kerry, and tried to make some sense of the mess my life had been turned into. I had a manic level of energy that kept me walking without respite all day every day anywhere. The Poor Laws, the Orwellian titled Social Security Laws, refused my pleas. I had voluntarily left paid employment in the United States: teaching the composition of creative writing for a pack of cigarettes a day in a university I was otherwise barred from attending. Normally doleful farmers laughed as freely as children when I tried to explain.

On borrowed money I arrived in Yorkshire, in the middle of its economic destruction. I could laugh, most callowly, at anything. Life was more and more hilarious. So many people still believed that their ordered lives held something precious and genuine, that there was just reward for sacrifice and effort. And believed that this was a law of nature. Then I heard that the borrowed money was being claimed back in the most brutal manner; it was being claimed back against royalties on the simple, solitary book that had been published four years before and on account of which I had first been sent to a US university that was absolutely innocent of the promises made in its name.

I made a friend in Yorkshire, one of the many Presbyterian ministers who needed a helper with an energy level of the near insane. There was a healthy spell of work, of calmness, of responsibility, of sanity. I could watch and analyse what was happening around me, external to me or my inner cares. With detachment I watched poverty spread like a blight across the land. It had nothing to do with me.

It was very late on a Thursday night in a village close to Barnsley. The shops in the village were unlit, and open. In the darkness groceries were dispensed on credit. But there was a colleagueship between miner and grocer, a bond. This business of charity and credit was treated as a transaction that was outside their friendship, took place in another realm, and could not affect the bond of friendship. As if the roles could have been reversed and no one would have noticed, that this was neither charity nor credit but joint human effort in the battle to survive. It was, most literally, a family of effort they had been born into, and were unaware of it, unaware of how far their concerns reached out and held each other. It was a well woven web about them and their lives. They made small jokes, and laughed lightly with each other. Things that I could not understand. In some manner I was omitted. I felt that. They could not all be wrong, in Ireland, the US, in England. They could not all be wrong.

I asked to borrow my friend's car for a few minutes. I drove to Barnsley, bought a bottle of whiskey and drove to my friend's flat. There I wrote a final goodbye note of thankfulness and laid it under the untouched bottle of Scotch. Then I drove about and found a by-lane in the moors.

The moment I switched off the engine there was peace; a harmonious peace in the order of nature. Not the coming deadly silence that I expected, not even the quietness of sleep — for nature wasn't sleeping. Just the absence of Man, of Humankind. I could have lived forever in that peace, but dawn was approaching.

I made the preparations and switched on the engine. Its noise raped everything of harmony in the night. I stood outside the car and smoked a cigarette. It had then the utilitarian function of making me breathe more deeply, which I found I was a little reluctant to do. Then I sat into the car and slammed the door tight. After a curious moment I checked the digits on my watch, but they appeared not to move at all. I took it off and shook it. The digits had moved.

Very slowly. Nothing was happening and it was taking an eternity to happen. I put down the back of the seat and tried to stretch out comfortably. It was cold in the car. Just the maddening noise of the engine and the cold and my inability to find a comfortable position. But soon it would be all over for all time. I was willing to go through this sacrifice for that happiness.

The clock on the dashboard moved not at all. And I kicked the fucking thing with rage. This should happen quickly. It should not loiter. Rage and anger and hate for so many people, all people, all things literally shook my body, an uncontrollable fiendish rage, and I hammered the heel of my shoe into the stupid dashboard clock that personified all. But the rage ebbed, and I regretted the expense I had just caused my friend. My right eardrum popped, and the engine's noise seemed to soar. All my mind and body fretted into agitation against that cursed noise that would not let me die in peace. That I had to suffer so to die. That I was not to die in the silence of the night was some epitaph on life, on *all* life that must all face this tumultuous, truculent, this deadly still and unquiet moment. But *all* my sadness and rage had left me. I remember that.

When I woke up in hospital only the sadness, as an unbearable depression, returned. *I could not even die.* The futility and depression flooded my eyes; and *I could not even cry*. A nurse showed me to myself in a handmirror and I saw myself unquestionably and disappointingly alive. My skin was the colour of red hot fire.

Later I learned the story of the curious dogs and their frightened whinings, the routine business of my friend scouring the countryside with colleagues, miners and farmers. It *was not even* a new experience for them, not during this period of virtual civil war in the mining areas of Great Britain. The boots kick-kicking in the car windows with experienced haste and ease, the undoing of the door lock, the resuscitation of breath, the roadside, the hard faces that were so far gone in their own unquiet despair that they *even* sympathised, and had nothing to say against me for the effort and strain I had caused them. Nowt, nowt at all. The noble kindness of simple words from these who live harsh lives, and put no stock, none at all, in promises.

Without knowing how or why I found I was telling all this to Lia squatted next to me on the floor. The bottle was hardly touched and I was telling her everything I had promised myself never to tell her. But I had promised first never again to lie. They are real and very vital experiences, the lies we tell ourselves. And they have, always, the unstoppable consequences of our own perdition to ourselves.

But my story, for all of its truth, had no fantasy of Brazilian exaggeration or brilliance in it. And she didn't like it. Her face was aghast, and she said she didn't want to hear any more, she didn't care, she didn't want to listen. She said it was unfair of me to tell her. And all the while both her hands were kneading mine with the gentleness of a distressed mother.

I said I once knew a cat who carried a walking stick when he went out walking on the mountains before breakfast each morning, and a smile broke through the sadness of her face, and there was forgiveness and there was love again in her eyes. She wanted to hear stories of talking cats, stories of the wildest fantasy, to take joy joy joy from the day, from any source, to create pleasure against the harsh act of living. Maupassant, and the story of the necklace had broken her heart when she was a girl. She had cried for days, and Yara too. For that life wasted in toil for a bauble, a real parable, but Yara wouldn't forgive Maupassant for not continuing the story. Oh was there somewhere in the world a true sequel lying unpublished? What was the truly insane Maupassant telling us from that perspective of the world?

I don't know, except that sometimes story-tellers must end their stories where they would otherwise begin, because only the listener can imagine the untidiness of the always shabby end life brings to all things; perforce.

But I promised to tell her stories and to watch over her while she drifted away in her own time into sleep.

Contented, she undressed and got into bed, sitting up in it in expectancy, and settled the pillows and sheets about her. I sat next to her and held her hands and told her the story of the fish that didn't know it was wet. But the metaphor didn't work too well, so I told her of the sweet little bird who didn't know she could fly and tried to walk, chump chump chump, across the sky. She fell like a stone. But just as she was about to hit the earth she saw a cat waiting. She panicked and madly flapped her wings in fright and lo! she sailed away with the greatest of ease, with just a little effort, into her natural element of freedom and happiness over lands and seas, living like a rich man, always in the best of seasons and dining off the ripest of the fresh spring fruits. And sometimes she would feel maternal if she saw a hungry, bedraggled old cat scratching for a meal and she'd catch a fish and drop it down to him, even though she didn't really, really, like cats, she couldn't help feeling sorry for them, sometimes.

My heart was not in the story-telling. Every time I lost sight of her eyes, looked at some detail of her face, looked at her hands in trust in mine, I was too aware that she was just at the beginning of her life, and I was just at the end of mine.

There are moments of eternally deep hatred in my life, when I truly wish a God was responsible for all of creation, that I should stand in front of Him in judgement, and spit in his face, for the eternal diversities and novelties of pain He created, the most sickening, bloodied, random, casual, deliberate sufferings He created in the universe He created for the habitation and experience of his love, the inescapable agony innately placed in life, as if His paradise could ever make up for it, the madness of this doctrine, the stupid madness of it, that He could undo the past of our experienced lives, ever retract or cancel or undo even the most singular and exponentially tiny, private hurts in our minds, and the universal encyclopaedia of our living torments, the inalterable cruelty of the human condition, experience, existence, that He created, for us.

But mercifully I stayed silent, and then I noticed she was already asleep, her head nod nodding to fall to her right. I was confident in my handling of her, and settled her down in the bed. She mumbled a little and I quietly hushed her. Then I undressed myself and lay beside her. She was breathing so evenly, so comfortably. I cuddled her to me and placed my hand on her stomach. Her breathing went long, longer, deeper, and for an amused moment I thought it might even catch on a snore. I lay in enchantment for a long, blissful time; and finally lost it, reluctantly, to sleep.

For how long I don't know. Her skin was soaked with sweat. My arm was gripped in her fists and her legs were kicking as wildly as a stallion's. And she was still fast asleep. Exactly the same as the previous night. I pushed my shoulder up to give her more leeway with my arm, and tried with my other hand to reach to her knees. Her thigh muscles were bundled fast, and with the strength of their tension, and the sweat, it was impossible to massage or squeeze some relaxation into them. I couldn't reach her knees without fear of slipping and so break my arm on my own weight. So I lay back and worked my hand about to her forehead and caressed it, and wiped the sweat off with my fingers, time after time, again and again. I had no idea what to whisper into her ear to address and quieten her dreams and nightmares. If only Maria were here. Alone, I was reduced to the banality of whispering 'relax' into her ear. And she showed no signs, of irritation or ease, to guide me. She finished as before, reaching to roughly massage the backs of her knees, but this time I left my hands on her, wherever they were, and pressed them softly against her body. Without waking she finished, and turned to lie into me, as if she had shrunk in stature, nestled against me and resumed her sleep.

I slept fully, and when I awoke she was still sleeping soundly. I passed the time making up a story for her. Of a mouse in Amsterdam who dreamed of being an elephant in Africa. An enormous, huge elephant. While all the other little baby mice were asleep he lay awake and dreamed of being a huge elephant in Africa when he grew up. And he told one or two of the other little mice of his dreams and they betrayed his confidence to the big mice and the big mice said he needed a doctor. The doctor said he was going to put him in a mouse asylum. This was a place run by mice for mice with strange dreams. There he met really strange mice; some wanted to be like cats and dogs and even humans. But they could see no point in being an elephant in Africa. In Brazil, yes, that would get attention, but not in Africa. So he quickly gave up the idea and they let him out again. The little mouse grew up with mice who were real mice and very proud of it they were too. And when they grew up the clever ones found good places in churches and banks and businesses and found mouse wives and mouse mistresses and commenced saving cheese and bread for their mousey old age.

One night, wandering about the alleys of Amsterdam and dreaming of being an elephant in Africa, the little mouse met a witch mouse. She said she could make him as big as he wanted to be. As big as a cat, as big as a dog, as big as a human, even as big as an elephant. But only if he gave her a kilo of Camembert. Genuine Camembert. A whole kilo. More than a normal mouse ever sees in one lump sum in a lifetime. So he scrimped and he saved and he went without and he did amazing things for bits of Camembert. Then he got it. The day came and he had it all. A kilo of genuine Camembert, all in one piece. He had grown old in all the hard years he'd spent trying to get it all together, and he had neglected many necessary provisions in his own life, in his quest for the magic kilo of Camembert. He lived in a poor house in a poor neighbourhood with other poor mice who were dulled, rude and dreamless in their detritus, cramped lives. A lot of implacably hungry mice-cats were always pawing about the mouse holes, making tempting offers, looking for a free mouse. Plus he had to wearily and continuously fend off the envious and greedy grabbings of the mice who were brutalised and vulgar, and callowed into a snout-minded mentality, just like Sylvia, relentlessly petty in their gross avarice, just like the mice comfortably ensconced in secure places. He had one or two silent friends, eccentrics, in his life, and with an exasperation of human proportions he despised almost all other mice. As a type he couldn't stand them, and dreamed and dreamed, dreaming himself almost insane, of being an elephant, an immense, a huge elephant, in Africa.

'What are you thinking about?' Lia asked. There she was; awake, as fresh as spring, as young as spring. Traces of a child's unfocused curiosity after sleep lingered about her.

'If you like I'll tell you a story,' I said. But no, she said. I had last night and they were so boring she'd fallen asleep immediately listening to them. I commended her on her morning pleasantness, and she teased and coaxed and enticed me into her happiness with promises of pleasures and of sex that not even Yara knew about. Yara could do any thing she wanted with a man. She never in her life had more than one man a night — that was said for my eavesdropping punishment alone — but she had studied books and she could do mysterious and strange things with men. Yara knew a way to keep a man rigidly hard and making love to her for at least three hours.

'Maria has a beautiful breakfast prepared,' I said, in my

own manner of morning pleasantness, succumbing, and she looked at me distrustfully, her mind and body working headstrong towards a more heated passion, and soon had me making love to her. She had me on top, but there was never any doubt as to who was in charge of this orchestrated pleasure. It is a most benign way to commence the day. She was always obedient, — when in bed — most forwardly anxious to be obedient, and manipulative, benignly, in the heat of her headstrong, loving manner; eager to love and to be loved in return.

In this regard she was similar to most of the normal women I have known, though I cannot, not even over a lifetime, extend this poll sampling to one hundred and forty-seven. Unfortunately. Though, if I may say so, and with becoming modesty, so to speak, I am just less than a handful short.

After we'd showered, before we went down to breakfast, she stopped me in the doorway. A lot, a great lot, of the worn tiredness had gone from her eyes. She had again the lovely eyes of a young woman on the verge of her greatest beauty. Yet not quite. But with gravity she told me I was safe now. The past could not reach me, unless I reached back to bring it, here, into the present. I could hear Maria's influence, and advice, in her voice. I promised. I said the past was a library, a private encyclopedia, in my mind, but not a presence.

Yet she had stumped me; there was a feeling of being diminished, of being too easily read, too easily changed. She had to alter me. I understood that. We each had to alter and change and accommodate each other into our joint life.

And her eyes were so much less tired, so much. They were young and radiant and healthy, as a young woman's should be, fresh. Almost all of the puckered worry lines had faded magically away.

Ten days later, on a Friday morning, we were married in the Church of Our Lady of the Assumption, New Orleans, Louisiana. This church is a one room timber shack on the banks of the Mississippi. Inside are huge, coloured cardboard movie-set replicas of St Peter's Basilica, Rome. Inside and out. You stand in front of these and get photographed, with the Pontiff smiling behind you. The ethical dishonesty of it disturbed Lia, though she smiled happily enough for the photographer, who was also the minister. All this is a rationalised state of affairs in privatised churches, in their infancy, operating in the free market.

Later that evening, in our hotel suite, Lia broke down looking at the photographs, and wept, and destroyed the photographs. She was inconsolable. I quelled it, somewhat, but couldn't bring back the joy, by a whispered promised to marry her again, in Brazil, in a proper church. But I missed the point of her sadness, then. Didn't know its depth and its loneliness; the missed friends, the missed past, the gaining of the knowledge that our emotions are communal, that others must partake of our life, else it is barren; and inconsolably sad, as sad and as comically sad as a funeral without mourners. Unwisely I viewed the entire event as stress management and control in the startling changes that were overtaking my life.

'Maria has a beautiful breakfast prepared,' I said again. And during that ritual breakfast of banterings and good humour I learned that Maria had three permanent guests. One was a woman who sold cigarettes in the Square Lisboa, another was an old man, an ex-lawyer who made a sharp living buying and selling US dollars on the street, but mostly near the magnificent doorway of the sumptuous Villa Rica Hotel. The third was a young Frenchman, but old, much older than his years. He had a disability pension from some European military force, but apparently not the French. He mulled about during his silent days, refused all alcohol until six pm and then drank himself into a stupor on cheap, illegal, Indian rum. Maria's other and infrequent guests were casual artisans on their way from place to place looking for work.

It was Lia's dream to one day have a home like this, to own a hotel like this; a dilapidated tenement slum. Meantime, we could live here on a month to month basis for two dollars a day. There were subtleties Maria wanted to resolve with Lia, mainly her sociability with Sylvia, and also Yara and the other girls. This they could best do alone while they cleaned up the breakfast room and commenced their cleaning of the house. I went out to walk about the streets.

At my favourite stone bench I sat down to take my ease and had my first cigarette of the day. But this was the first day, in almost four years, that I was on the streets, anywhere, without sedatives. The triumphant confidence in me was growing, minute by minute, like a strength of character. The detoxification-high. I sat and basked in it. It is a cool rationality, a level-headed realism, totally untrustworthy, and well known to anyone who has ever touched active insanity. In fact it is the same.

When they'd taken me from casualty to the psychiatric ward in the Yorkshire hospital I just lay back and let images and ideas, of fact and fantasy, float impartially around my mind. There were still many things fretting and disturbing in the weave of my mentality, especially the trauma of the American university experience. I proved with documents that it was not a hallucination. But a lady doctor told me bluntly and with great authority that the story was a lie, a nonsensical, stupid lie, and the documents, therefore, were petty, idiotic, worthless forgeries. With the medication they were giving me it was very easy to get angry or sad, to release emotion. Emotions yawed like a ship in a rough sea, there was a fluidity, an extra viscosity, in them. Unfortunately I became too angry, far too angry with the bitch, and was transferred to a lunatic asylum, called by some other name.

Less than a day later and I had a better understanding of the power of psychiatry. I met Napoleons, Churchills, Kennedys, men from families of great wealth, men from universities of great fame. And these were the least of the inhabitants in this realm of delusion and illusion, a gallery of historical and famous and wealthy characters with the exact accents and mannerisms of their faked identities. They were uncomfortably too similar to too many people outside, whose pretensions may not be so exaltedly exhibited, but whose intensity is of the same order. More, there was a closed ward within this closed hospital, for men, mostly old men, suffering from the consequences of manic sexual repression, heterosexual and homosexual. Their language and gestures and actions were of a crepuscular, numbing foulness; unknowable to any beast other than human. But, once seen and heard, is instantly recognisable in our own mind, previously unworded, previously unimagined, previously unreleased. But there, always there, instantly recognisable. I was anxious to get out. I was level-headed, frightened, and sane. I contacted the lady doctor and apologised and asked her to make some telephone calls, at my expense, which would be covered by my friend, a respected minister of religion.

She came to visit me two days later, smiling and most definitely, with sophisticated strain, treating me as an equal. She said it was a wonder I hadn't gone mad. She said it with a great maquillage of a smile. I smiled one back. To carry, alone, such a trauma for such a long time was the only self-inflicted wound I'd committed against myself. I could have gotten very angry, again, with the casual stupidity of her Delphic utterances, and the arrogance of their delivery. But it was better to pander and please her rather than reason with her. She was that kind. I knew that then. But there was so little common sense and civility in people, generally, she said. And you ought to fuckin know, I thought, you at least ought to read yourself back into the human race you medicate with such inept results.

Only this morning she'd discovered that in a village in Hampshire a retirement villa for the wealthy aged was sold out the day it opened. Yet it had the same leafy, relaxed name as this place, a somesuch name such as Roedean Lawns. She phoned to tell them this and suggest that they quickly rename their villa, but was told to mind her own business, that cheap jokes were not appreciated, that their clients had earned their wealth and were fully entitled to enjoy its benefits unhindered by cranks and further calls would be considered harassment and reported to the police. So she put the phone down. That was the world.

But only when it collides with you, I thought, and wished more power to the guy who had rebuffed her blunt meddling. The contemporary historical figure who was her 'role-model' was obvious, and I was so glad one of her own kind had put her down. She would see to it that my release papers were processed with dispatch and I could then visit her as an out-patient in the general hospital. Meantime, I was to get a private room and the freedom of the grounds.

Thus I waited, day by day, for the release letter. Every morning at seven I went to the main gates and helped the porter sort and deliver the mail. Naturally I was asked to do more and more. It quickly amounted to a full-time job. I mentioned this to one of the doctors and he said he'd see what he could do about it. Later I discovered this only went onto my dossier as a sign of rehabilitation.

When the release letter arrived I recognised it and slipped it into my pocket. I was waiting for the doctor to organise my work into a full-time job. Again I asked him, told him my fear of being released into unemployment. Then I was told. I shouldn't really think about working for a little while, although I was doing just that: working. I'd get a sickness benefit payment once a fortnight at the post office, and I ought to relax and enjoy it. Another joker. If madness is not infectious, it is at least a compelling pattern, a vortex of emotions into a predictable mode of behaviour. And this joker in white, this Son of Freud, was twirling away inside, licking his fingers and turning over the pages of someone else's dossier.

So I gave up and decided to slip the release letter back into the office mail. Very early the next morning I went down to the main gates for a chat and a cup of tea with the porter. He was a civil, aged man and normally did his humble job with rare aplomb and contentment. This morning he was near berserk. The postman had dropped off two fully packed sacks of mail. There was a letter for every inmate; some, many, most, hadn't received a single letter in years. All the letters were of identical weight with identical postmarks. I sorted them, found the one for me and put it into my pocket. Inside the main building I ripped it open. Incredibly it contained a major credit card, instructions on all of its many benefits, and a notification that a Personal Identification Number would follow shortly. I ripped open another, the same. I went down to the furnace-room, bagged the letters, and went back to the porter and showed him. To keep life quiet we ought to burn them all. It was against the law, but otherwise all hell would break loose and we'd be worked footless all day. Plus the office staff sending all the stuff back, and then be accused of interfering with the mail.

'Please do it, Paddy,' he said, in despair. 'Please just fucking do it now.'

I waited until after the next weekend for my PIN to arrive before slipping my release letter back into the office mail. While thousands of pounds in PIN numbers fed the furnace. Thanks to an uppity retirement villa in Hampshire. And the computer amassed appetite of a credit card company for the wealthy aged.

At nine o'clock the head orderly called me to his office, thanked me for my work about the place, gave me a backdated unemployment and sickness cheque, and added some personal money of his own.

With the mighty dominion of a scribbled name I was discharged. From total dependence on others if I wanted a cup of tea or the light switched on in my room; from an institution whose primary efforts had been to undermine, subvert, and abolish my belief in my own judgements, and replace it with conformed, mesmerised hypocrisy; I was now discharged into total and unprepared dependence on my old, unreliable self. From an institution where all of the doctors, without exception, were looping in ever smaller loops at the end of their already antiquated learning curve, had an appalling success rate in their profession, and were utterly dependant for their meagre success on the effects of the pharmaceuticals to whose recipients they so obviously felt a moral superiority. No physician would ever feel so about a sick or injured patient. About the institution, about the primitive but academically structured shamanism, I have only negative things to say. But I admire the tablets, greatly.

I went around making my goodbyes. There was even a whisper of sadness in the leave-taking; the loss of a security, no matter how tenuous. Despite the jokes from the orderlies that it must be Uncle Joe Freud's anniversary if amnesties were being handed out. At the main gates I chatted with the porter, received his blessing for all the best in the future, and caught the first bus into town.

I re-met my minister-friend and we agreed I should go back to a spare room in his house, for a while. Over the next three weeks we had many long talks and I think he lied to me, just once. Yet I treated it as unforgivable betrayal, and thereafter held him in my secret contempt. Although I, definitely and deliberately, lied to him, continuously.

Despite all the talking, to doctors and to the minister, despite the counselling, the medication, Thorazine or less, the old winding tension began again to coil itself slowly within me. Without respite; tightening, tightening, another presence growing inside my mind, inside my own reasoning. Inside my heart, figuratively, literally. I could gain no release from the growing pressure of this tension readying itself to explode inside my skull, within my heart, within, deeply within, the mesh of my mentality. Except by bouts of alcoholism, heavy doses of. And the wild beasts of hatred and foulness and unutterable joy in my mind were given their uninhibited romps of vile imaginings of revenge and retribution. The alcohol calmly led them out; and slowly released them, from the primeval depths of my mind, anxious to stalk, eager for the clash of beast felling beast, the smell of hot flowing blood, the bloodied snarl of victory, the re-assertion of my primacy in this world, in all of the literal, grunting sense of that word. To expunge the hatred within me in the scurrying and the thrashing bouts of death in the primeval forest of emerging, ruthless, human life and dominance over all life. And I could hurl and smash the bottle against the wall and rage, rage; rage against my limping, wounded life. And sob, silently, intensely, in the silence of myself.

Once, doing this, I used the bottle left untouched on my

Night of Resolution. The resolution that led to my assault on life. Because the first one to the car, a farmer, and not a stranger to the taking of life had noticed the birds. Kill, said the farmer, take life, pluck life, human life, as silently as you will, yet the birds will rise. A flutter of wings, a hovering in the air, if human life is taken. No bird remains at rest in the vicinity. All are afright the moment human life is stolen. So quoted the minister, and I think he lied. Not directly for his own ends, but those of theism. Despite his goodness he was, like the psychiatrists, bound first to the eternal truths of his profession more than the transient truths of an individual client.

But of the consequences he was correct. My ability to value truth above falsehood vanished. Each became a utility, its value relative to its utility. But perhaps everyone, from birth, already knows this. I was merely late, very late, catching up. Yet it remains with me, as an absolute flaw in the human species, that the truth of the human condition is hidden in folklore, in the celestial ichors of literature, and is not a natural imperative in daily life, where falsehoods are natural, unconscious, fluent and convenient; and essential to survival.

That is why I should rather live alone with books. I needed a modest, humble job and a quiet place to read and to sleep. And, yes; perchance to dream. This I mumbled to the bottle and to my friend. It was true, yet devious.

The clock on the dashboard had been smashed, and perhaps the hands had been altered in the smashing, otherwise there was no explaining my living presence. But I had kicked the glass directly and flatly with the heel of my shoe. The hands of the clock would have been squashed against the clock-face. But I swore my thanks to the farmer and his colleagues, to the psychiatrists. Then my friend left the room while the beasts began their prancing grotesques of midnight cavortings in the primeval, silent forests of my mind. And all injustices to me were most bloodily avenged in a joyous litany of snarls and the ripping of teeth into flesh.

Late the following afternoon, to mutual amusement, I was told that aged Britons were magically proliferating, and that a villa for them in southern Portugal needed a general factotum; porter, kitchen help, maintenance man. The minister had arranged the job and the flight.

Signing-off at the employment exchange, receiving my last welfare cheque, I deliberately exposed my gold card. The mouse-eyes of the clerk looked as if they'd just seen, direct from Africa, a huge, an immense, elephant materialise before them.

Now, years later, here I was, on my favourite stone bench in Itaqui, smoking and contemplating how that massaged gold card might bring unknown joys into Lia's young life, before my aged one ended.

Then, I used my dole-cheque to open a bank account and set-up a direct debit mandate on the card. I used the minister's respectable address. And once a month in Portugal I used the card, and each month fully repaid the debt, as required. All this, to no preconceived, set plan. Just a quirk of my curiosity. But I had thus extended my credit to such proportions that my card caused instant and noisy orgasm in the cash dispenser the moment I slid it in.

It was all so long ago, so far away, from this stone bench in Itaqui. Here, on this bench, for the first time ever, the overpowering anger came to me in sobriety; the permanence of my hatred for those who had betrayed my life and my life's striving for some petty gain of their own, too petty for them ever to acknowledge or explain. From Lord Mayor to the most dim apparatchik. But the demons that stalked my mind would now learn to stalk elsewhere.

I got up and walked, passed the stupid Corkman who allowed his dog to bark at me and OK if I were that stupid I'd too need a dog with some brains to take care of me. Then passed Sylvia's attempt to catch my attention, past the Convento do Carmo, down the thronged boulevard that led somewhere. I was hating people, for the stupidity in the way they walked, the stupidity of their rush, push, shove and arrogance, for the stupidity of not looking where they were going, their attitude that they owned the very world, including the pavement. They weren't wired, they weren't hyped to reality, goddamn them, and I turned from one street to the next and was turning into another when a street-child caught my hand and said, no, no, Gringo, you can't go in there, they're the death slums. And even if they were, even if I found death in those slums for the price of my worn shoes, or just to dissipate some hoodlum's anger, I would not there find a rape of my life and dreams more stupidly executed and more cruel than had been casually perpetrated upon me in my own erstwhile country, and by its paid representatives. That I had not sought retribution now amazed me.

I gave the kid a few hundred Cruzeiros, and turned back to the relative safety of the main street.

It is historic, when you walk through the ruins of your life, when you realise: I let this happen, and then I paid the price of allowing it to happen; paid not just emotionally, mentally, physically, but with the irredeemable time, all of that long and now dead time of my life; and more, and, yes, the talent, however modest, of my only life. Laid to waste.

In the Mansion House of the capital city of a west European country. I shook the hands of men whose lack of a sense of honour would embarrass the Mafia's lowest hoodlum. I know the arrogant pushing, shoving, heaving, blind greed and pellucid egos of the simian, elbowing mentalities that rule in the death slums. If only a street-child had caught my hand in Dublin.

I found the US consul in an unguarded office above the local brewery. He was a pleasant, relaxed man and told me what I needed to know, and gave me the necessary application forms.

Coming back across the Square I saw Lia standing with Sylvia and the Gorgons and the waifs. Strangely, Yara was in some embarrassment and was too preoccupied to notice me. She held her closed fist to her mouth in a manner identical to Lia's. When I approached Lia smiled at the group, straining most of all to smile at Yara, then moved away and came to me.

'Maria is very strong,' she said. If we were to live in the Hotel Napoli Lia and I had to renounce our casual friendship with Sylvia and the girls, and our transactions must be kept to matters of proper, correct business, only. So said Maria. But it was none of Maria's goddamn business, I said. But it suited Lia to go along with it. It separated her from Sylvia, safely separated her from Sylvia.

'We can do that without anyone's permission,' I said, and walked her back to the group. 'We're going to America. Soon,' I said. Lia's hand jammed tight on mine with a nightmarish force, and her body strained to pull me away. Her head bowed as if she were looking sideways behind her. Yara's face opened in shock, and her expression then slowly changed into an open, bewildered, lost sadness. She looked away from me to look at Lia's face, but Lia was turning and pulling me away. We walked on.

'I love Brazil,' she said, 'I'm never leaving Brazil. Never.'

'We're not leaving. We're going on vacation.'

'Where can you find such money?'

'Where can you find a passport, Lia, Leila, Leticia? What circus did your mother work for?'

She laughed, a child's amused laughter, wide-mouthed as a child. But the young woman quickly came to the fore.

'It never mattered to me,' she said, 'But only Sylvia can get a passport for me. Or it will take months and months and be very expensive. For you.' Just like the mountain cat, she could suddenly pass all moral and financial responsibility onto me, as if my unilateral actions had led her innocently up to this impasse, and it was my responsibility to therefore take up her burden. I could never quite understand the logic, but I knew she was right.

She went on to Maria's, and I returned to Sylvia. I took her aside and told her what I wanted.

'I'll make it up to you, Sylvia,' I lied.

'She could have married an aristocrat,' said Sylvia, 'When she first came here with nothing, nothing, I told her. She could marry the Chief of Police, even a young man from a wealthy family. I told her. But she was never like Yara, never knew when to be obedient to get on in life. Never wanted to learn to play the game.'

I was staggered at this philosophical turn of expression. Coming from Sylvia. Did she understand what she was saying?

'I'll make it up to you, Sylvia. I swear to God.'

She stood and looked at me, her acquisitive greedy eyes searching every aspect of mine.

'What did you do in Europe?'

'Many things.'

'Don't fuck with me. What did you do?'

'I was a writer,' I said. And to my amazement she didn't laugh.

'You had books published?'

'One. Yes.'

'Did you pay for it to be published?'

'No.'

'Your name is in some index, some directory, some list, of European writers?'

'I don't know.'

'Your passport,' she said, 'What is your profession on your passport?'

'It doesn't list a profession.'

'When you applied for it, when you filled in the Brazilian visa forms, what occupation did you claim?'

'Writer.'

'Tell me your name, your real name.'

I told her, but she could not understand it. I had to write it down for her. And doing this I noticed that she now believed me. More, there was genuine respect and deference in her demeanour towards me.

'You have been to prison, you are a fugitive criminal?'

'Don't be silly.'

'If you are lying you are the one who is stupid. Very stupid.'

'I'm old enough to regret my stupidities, Sylvia. I don't repeat them.'

'A month from now I want a thousand US dollars from you.'

'Impossible, Sylvia.'

'If you have a thousand dollars a month from now I want it.'

'You'll get it, if I have it.'

She put out her hand, and I had to shake the bloody thing.

'I've never believed a European in my life,' she said, and walked away.

I was lost, bewildered, left suddenly standing without purpose like an abandoned idiot. I went to sit down, floundering in my mind to create some purpose for my listless actions. I took out a cigarette, couldn't stand the sight of the bloody thing and threw it away unlit. A street-child appeared from nowhere and grabbed it and scampered away.

I needed home, I needed Lia's presence, needed her presence to refocus me to myself.

I was passing the Corkman without realising it when he said something. I didn't catch it, except its malice. When I looked at him there was a sneer on the bastard's face.

'I'm glad you have a dog,' I said, 'I'm glad you've finally found a fucking friend in your miserable fucking life. Cos that's all you'll ever get for a friend: a subservient dog. Obedient friends don't come in human form, you shithead.' He was too old, too limp-brained, too selfish to understand, but he looked utterly gobsmacked and even his mongrel was quiet. And yet I didn't mean to hurt the man. I would have said the same to any lamppost had it attracted my attention.

In the dining room of the Hotel Napoli, Lia and Maria sat like two judges. I looked from one to the other.

'I hope you are a serious man,' Maria said. I looked at Lia. Maria stood up and left, walking slowly, the deportment of a judge on the tremulous verge of reaching a decision. In the atmosphere of the room I didn't feel it was my place to sit down. I stood. Lia looked at me, at my eyes, and spoke the name she had given me. Then she lowered her head.

'What are going to do with me in the United States?' she asked.

'I'm going to marry you.'

Her head snapped up and she stared at me, happiness, joy, and beauty budding from her face like miracles.

'For ever?' she asked.

'For ever.'

She stood up from the table, the beauty of the first dawn of creation aglow in her. And she said such words of love to me that they tasted like flowers of Summer on fire in sparkles of colours in my mind, made me feel beautiful and treasured and unique, made me proud, made me feel as joyous as a child, joyous as a man, made the innocence of creation come alive again and quicken in me: made me taste the ultimate joy of life; that there is joy, there is joy, incarnate, in the universe.

It was a creation of wonder; of silent aeons of paradise; a rapture of happiness. She spoke words of love that were the heart and soul and life of joy; an enchantment of emotions, young and slenderly tender and vulnerable; sonnets of basic words of wonder, trust, and need; the sacred reciprocities of all our minds would ever hold. All our worlds went silent, our universe at its final, blessèd peace; while yet we lived.

A lifetime's journey to meet this moment, and all before was now redundant; a limbo of mere sentient life. This moment now lives on in my mind, as an eternity of joy, of wonder, as beauteous as the dawn on the first day of creation.

The first sound I later heard, dimly, coming from that other world outside us, was a timid knock on the Hotel door. When I opened it I must have been smiling. There was the quiet and shy Yusmely. She was on the verge of a bashful smile and put out her hand to greet me. I shook her hand and felt something pass into my palm. 'Go there anytime. We have no English lessons tonight,' she said, and Lord, but the little girl was trying to speak her Brazilian in a Dublin accent; the very height of esoteric, cosmopolitan chic to her. I nodded, and she let her smile flow, and she turned, and showed me the swank and jilt of her departing, shimmying, court-jestering, sexy walk.

In my hand was a hotel room key. The Villa Rica Hotel, suite 18. I just pocketed the thing and went back into the dining room. Even Maria, dour distrust ready to lurk, and yet set free into her element of the wise grandmother, was swamped into sedate, grandmotherly contentment by the solidity of Lia's bouncing, smiling delight. And Maria went, as she always did when words of dampening caution failed her, to cook a celebration meal. Between holding my hand with a manic force, and wanting to go and talk to Maria and exchange secret whispers and coming back to me, Lia did not know whether to sit or stand or talk or just scream and laugh. She was so relaxed she was weightless. And I thought it best to leave her to Maria's wise ministrations and company, leave them to the open privacy of all they wanted to counsel and say and advise and exchange with each other. So, before dark, it was best to do some errands and return in twenty or thirty minutes.

I went upstairs and slit the gold card out of its hiding place in the inner cardboard base of my holdall. Then I walked to the Villa Rica Hotel.

My 'gringoness' got me past the armed guards and the doormen without any hindrance. At first there was nothing amiss in suite 18, not the bathroom, bedroom, dayroom. I looked behind cushions, opened drawers, the Gideon bible, even lifted up the mattress. In the bathroom I tipped the toe-lever on the garbage pail, and the top lifted. Nothing. I lifted the pail and taped inside the bottom recess was a manila envelope. Inside, written on toilet paper, were typed instructions on how to activate the passport. I shredded the instructions and flushed them. Of all the places on my body where I might conceal the envelope, there was none that wouldn't produce a bulge, and advertise I was hiding something, make that conspicuous to even a casual observer. This quandary was a test. I knew it instantly. I took the Gideon bible, held the envelope on the outside, and carried both out of the hotel, cursing myself for not having brought Maria's Taurus with me.

The doorman got me a cab. At Maria's he waited and I

brought out Lia. She was bemused and excited. Maria's gun was in my pocket. We drove across Itqui, on the cabdriver's advice, to an US style shopping mall near an area of high class apartments surrounded by a twelve foot wall topped with barbed wire. There were two security guards armed with automatic pistols at the single entry and exit control. I asked the cabdriver and he said some of these apartments cost as much as four hundred US dollars a month.

In the superb shopping mall we found a photographer's and had our photos taken, serious passport photos. Then Lia jumped on my lap and our most precious, happiest, most blessèd photograph of us together was snapped then; Lia sitting on my knee and smiling like the dawn of a sunrise even more beautifully alive than the tropically beautiful dawn of creation.

Within ten minutes we were back in Maria's, the door bolted and barred behind us.

Maria's extra special homeopathic sauce needed to naturally cool before reheating and there was time to spare. They wanted me to take a beer, a whiskey, to celebrate, but I wanted none of those things. I said I needed an clothes-iron, for some private items I wanted to press in my room. I held off Maria's and Lia's offering to do it for me, do it properly for me. But it was private; and I needed just ten minutes. So they bantered and badgered me and then allowed me to go upstairs with my precious little boy's secret that no woman in the world doesn't know about men the day she is born. Pretending to be chastened and abashed I went upstairs with the precious iron. And when I was there I realised I was missing the most vital piece of information. I plugged in the iron and went back down.

I had to take Lia away from Maria, and accept more of their humorous taunts about the trembling nerves of men when once they admit they need to be married.

But what I wanted to know was simply her name, her real first name, or the name she wanted: Lia, Leticia, Latitia, Lydia, Leila, what?

'It's Ilana,' she whispered, very seriously. 'It was the name of my father's mother.' Her face had become blank, utterly expressionless like a person totally lost in a distant memory. 'But don't tell even Maria, no one. Please. Not even Yara. She knows a million things, but not this. Only one, only one other person in the world knows my real name.'

I hugged her. And if I had held her a moment longer I would have cried for the innocence of the absolute trust she put in me. I whispered bounden promises of joy to her. I meant them. I meant them then. For fear of crying with happiness I couldn't look at her. I turned ungainly, unmannerly, loutishly away and stooped, and awkwardly went rapidly back upstairs.

In our room I followed the memorised instructions to activate the passport. For five seconds I put a cigarette lighter to the tip of a biro, held the biro between my middle and third fingers and pressed my thumb heavily and affirmatively on the shaft. Then swiftly I filled in all the necessary details, in the authoritative handwriting of a bureaucrat, on this new Irish passport. I put two sheets of heavy blotting paper under one page, another two over the page with the photograph, and covered these with a moistened handkerchief. Then I pressed the steaming iron onto the handkerchief and pressed with all my weight. When the handkerchief began to scorch and burn I waited a moment, then released my pressure and removed the iron. I gently quenched the odd burning embers on the totally scorched handkerchief. Then I let all set.

Out of anxiety I sat and smoked a cigarette, and another. And waited. I held the passport up by the corners and shook it gently. Nothing. Again I went to smoke and to wait. Again I picked up the passport and again shook it. The handkerchief and the paper slowly peeled off and dropped away. And there, on the page, was the magically arisen embossed stamp across the bottom of Ilana's photo. On other pages I repeated the procedure, and up came a Brazilian visa, another page and an Italian entry stamp, Rome airport.

I knew then, without doubt, what I was getting in to. I knew that then. And I knew it wouldn't lead to shovelling snow, or selling my blood, or teaching the writing of 'creative' literature for the pay of a pack of cigarettes a day. I knew, also, it might lead directly to my death, or to something worse. I did it for the most selfish reason I have ever experienced in my life; to bring joy to Ilana. I thought about that. Joy to Ilana was directly, thoroughly and totally, joy to me. It was one and the same joy. And fuck the world, fuck the rest of creation. I was going to make a goddamn buck, play the game of the bottom line where the ruthless and the greedy never finish last.

Yes, then, I was poor. Yes, then, I was alone. Yes, she saw me, she took me, and she loved me. She gave me all the great might and strength of her love. And yes: I was going to make her happy.

And yes: Fuck the rest of the creation.

I stood the passport, pages ajar, on the night-table. Then I picked it up again. I opened the Gideon bible to Ecclesiastes, a 'Book of the Apocrypha', and read: 'For I returned, and saw under the sun, that the race went not to the swift, nor the battle to the strong, nor bread to the wise, nor riches to the intelligent, nor favour to the skilled, but time and chance befalleth all.' Are these the words of God? I read on: 'A season for all things ... a time to kill and a time to heal, a time to break down and a time to recover, a time for war and a time for peace, a time to be born and soon the time to die ....' And so it went on. I settled and read all of Ecclesiastes, King James' edition, in ancient Portuguese. It was great, dramatic, wise writing, full of Brazilian invention and love of amazing beliefs. On the most magnificent page of this work of creative literature, this nationality-less, culture-less, ethos-less, ethnic-less, page of pure human literature, forged in cold white heat in the best manner of the best literature, the best art, I placed Ilana's passport, pages ajar.

I was too happy to be in Ilana's company, anyone's company. I paced the room. I had to force my happiness to allow me to leave my private world and go downstairs.

Yara, beautiful, gallant, delicious, bouncing Yara, eyes always bright with her natively quick and absorbing intelligence, was there. She was there; under the obvious sufferance and probation of Maria. And she had been crying. The dark puck of sadness was still under her smiling eyes. But Maria was utterly changed towards me; she was utterly deferential. She insisted on calling me 'Sir'. She turned herself into an obedient maid to me, and rebuked Ilana and Yara for their hysterical laughter at her behaviour.

Yara asked to shake my hand. Yara, she who had grabbed my buttocks with a savagely loving bite whenever she felt like it, now asked permission to shake my hand. And when she did so, she said it was her pleasure to meet me, she had never before met a writer. Immediately she asked: 'You are coming back? You'll bring Lia back?'

'I swear to you, Yara. Yes.'

She shook her head lightly from side to side, her eyes longing to know if I spoke the truth, then quietly, as she leaned forward to kiss me gently and quickly on my lips said: 'OK.'

I should have taken her more seriously, given her

worries direct and concentrated attention, and absolutely removed them, forever.

But Sylvia had blabbed. I had to immediately note that with grave concern, and doing so occupied my mind for a moment too long. That bitch.

Maria was in command. We had her extra special pasta, we ate meat; Brazilian steaks. We ate fish, long slivers of the white meat of a fish with all the magnificence of the Atlantic ocean in full roar in its taste. Maria, Maria who taught me to love proper food, exceeded excellence that night. We ate a banquet no king, pope, president has ever had. We ate with the ungluttonised, grateful relish of normal people presented with a feast. And we drank wine with every course, Ilana and Yara daughterly accepting Maria's watering of their wine, and drinking more than Maria approved of, while my glass, whenever I sipped it, was instantly replenished by Grandmama Maria. Grandmama Maria, ever ready to scowl at her spiritual granddaughters, was tipsy after a couple of glasses, and occasionally lost her soft Portuguese to her old Italian, and crossed many homonyms from Italian across into Brazilian and had Yara and Ilana roaring with uncontrollable laughter.

But every word, every gesture, the slightest thing, was, of itself, a feast. If only that evening had never ended. If only my life had ended in that feast of humanity that evening I would then have lived for eternity in paradise. There was paradise there that night; there was paradise. I have lied I have cheated I have stolen I have deceived I have betrayed I have killed human life. That is true. This is true: there was a feast and a paradise of humanity, of shared, mingled humanness, paradise, prodigal joy, that night. A happiness the author of Ecclesiastes shows no sign of ever even imagining.

The evening, the night, the feast, ended.

It ended without sadness, but with tired, sleepy happiness.

The moment after we came into our room she saw the passport. She hesitated, for a second like a cat in arrested motion, all nerves set in a stilled strain of energy ready to pounce. She picked the passport up slowly, cautiously, as if it might vanish if not shown reverence. She read it, gazed at it, curious amazement on her face as she again and again turned over page after page. Even her lips moved in expectation as she read this multilingual document of freedom, limited, to move. Her eyes turned to me and said: 'Your name is this? Kwin? Twin? And I am already your wife?'

'It's not my name. Someone I never knew gave it to me. It's the name on my passport. And you are my daughter.'

If cats in Kerry could smile they would smile as she smiled then.

'I'm not twenty-one,' she said, 'I'm nineteen.'

'You're seventeen, Ilana.'

She dipped her head and scowled companionably at me.

'But you are giving me your family name.'

'I have no family. You gave me my first name. I am giving you my surname.'

Thereafter, in private, she called me only by the name she had given me, and in public by my first name. In private I addressed her as Ilana; in public, Lia, Leila, latitia, layla, leela, but never Ilana. Together in private we were different people with a privacy and an intimacy, even of names, no one in the world ever knew of. Until now, until this, my betrayal of her, many years after I lost her.

She held the passport in both hands and shook it, and seemed to acquire a new confidence.

'This is wonderful,' she said. 'This is truly wonderful.' And sat on the side of the bed to recover herself. She noticed the book and leaned over to look at it.

'Ah! I know. I know,' she said and reached for it. 'You

want me to read this. I know what you want me to read. I know all of the bible.' And she reached to run a finger down the page and quoted "Enjoy life with the wife whom you love" Yes? That is beautiful. "Go! Eat your bread with enjoyment, and drink your wine with a merry heart, for God has already approved what you do." Oh I know all of this very well, almost by heart. I believe it, too. In a way.'

She was looking at the book, flicking slowly through the pages, and looking into memory. Once, she told me, Yara, who knew it all much better than she had said it was all ancient Jewish foreboding and the lonely, lifeless exaggerations of the desert, and Homer was better, more true. She didn't like her saying that, but Yara had been punished badly for saying it and she didn't approve of that either. She liked Homer and the bible equally. They enraptured something inside the mind, and the judgements, the exaggerations, didn't matter. It was human verisimilitude, she said. Anyway, she never understood what Yara had meant, and didn't want to ask her. She didn't want to appear less intelligent than her friend — they weren't so fast friends, then. Yara was intelligent, very intelligent. She could even read a book and talk to Sylvia at the same time.

She closed the book and put her passport, reverently, under it.

That night, feeling the ceaseless tossing of her soul as she lay in my arms, I told her the story of the mouse in Amsterdam. I was her child to her that night. She hugged me and petted me and encouraged me to imagine more, made me exaggerate more. The poor, the little, old, old mouse, sweating and half-dying and finally pushing the magical kilo of Camembert through the poor streets of the bad areas of beautiful Amsterdam. He was hungry, desperately hungry for just one morsel of cheese, any cheese, and desperately hungry, mad with a blinding, a consuming hunger, to be an elephant, yet.

Lo and behold! The mouse-witch turned him into an elephant. A big, a huge, an enormous elephant. His dream, his dreams had all come true. He was an elephant! A real Elephant!

Oh! He was so big. So big. He was delirious with happiness. Even his little toe was enormous. But people were screaming and running everywhere and he knew, oh God, they were going to set an elephant trap for him. The mouse witch had made a mistake. Why was she so dumb? She had only listened to half of what he said, the mouse-brained bitch. But he couldn't see her anymore. She was down there, just a mere speck, somewhere near his toe. She had all that cheese, a whole kilo of Camembert.

He wanted to go home. He was crying. He was too big. Some people stood and gawked at him like idiots in all his trembling, cold, vulnerable, unclotheable, undisguisable, giant nakedness. They were even looking at his enormous private parts and taking photographs, and he was blushing with embarrassment. He lifted his head in despair and a terrible noise like a trumpet came out of his huge nose. Then he charged; charged home, maddened out of his mind. But he couldn't get back into his little mouse-hole, where once he had been poor but happy and safe and secure except for his bloody mad dreams. He roared again, tried to put his trunk in through the door and the entire house collapsed. And out hopped an enraged, screaming cat and the mouse-elephant caught his breath in fright. Mad cats were running everywhere, screaming. His knees trembled. He lost his breath in fear and panic. He remembered telling her he wanted to be an elephant *in Africa*, the stupid mouse. That was his last bitter thought, before he broke down and fainted. But already Ilana was soundly sleeping in my arms.

Her nightmare came to her again that night. There was no change. She gripped my arm with a superhuman grip, her legs kicked and kicked, she sweated until she was awash in sweat. Only the broken words of her mumblings changed. Broken bits, broken sounds, of German, and not so frantic as before, and here and there a direct and plain sentence of schoolbook English.

The following morning I was wide awake, and fully rested after a long sleep, and still she slept on soundly. All tiredness was gone from her face. Not one single furrow on her face. She looked as young as she was, and even younger.

When she did awake she was instantly fully awake, alert and bright, had a thousand things to do, and endless realms of energy, and more, to do them.

Within minutes she was showered and dressed and ready to spin the entire world in her hands.

In minutes she completed the US visa application form and gave it and her passport and photos to me. Then we went downstairs and had a normal family breakfast with Maria and Yara.

Lia and Yara were going some places to do some things and I didn't have to ask if I wasn't wanted along. I was going to abuse my gold card, to buy flight tickets, and then to wait. If what I was sure would happen didn't happen, creation, with a vengeance, would soon fall on me.

Later, as the consul casually leafed through our applications and the passports and saw the gold card I'd accidentally left there he ignored it. But he quite naturally said 'What a beautiful daughter.' I thanked him, demurred, and finally said that her mother was recently deceased. I named a day and a date. For biblical verisimilitude. I said I appreciated I should have applied for the visa in Dublin. But the young are volatile, and she had picked up some paperback in some airport and now just had to see New Orleans, the most beautiful city in the US.

'I don't know,' he answered. 'Never been there.'

'I'll tell you when I get back.'

'Sure thing. What book was it anyway?'

Good shit. I hadn't been expecting this, and I should have been ready to expect anything. At least this.

'James Baldwin, I think.'

'Thought he was from New York.'

'Me too, but ...' And I shrugged, 'Young girls, you know...'

'Yeah,' he said, 'I appreciate that situation. I've got two of my own. I know, believe me.' But of course he didn't. Maybe as a father, but that's not knowing them at all; that's the silliest fools' gold in the valley. One day I'd have Yara bring him up to speed on this topic.

Then it crossed my mind that the story Yara told of the guy nearly splitting her in half was something I'd heard before, somewhere; perhaps I'd read something like it in one of Baldwin's books. But I couldn't locate the reference. But if it were, then Ilana would at least know of James Baldwin.

'Yeah,' he said again, 'They take a lot of understanding.'

Then he shifted back to business. He'd phone suite 18 at the Villa Rica as soon as he had received faxed permission to indent the visas. I tried to push for a little more conversation. He was of a genial disposition, but like so many expatriates who could not, for any of many reasons, fully assimilate into the host society, he had become afflicted with a self-boredom, a sort of introspection without reflection, a self-justifying indulgence, a premature, hapless senility in social intercourse, a constancy of repetition of old and ever modifying stories of fantasy and fact, of delusion, all thoughts quickly winding into total absorption of some personality or aspect of some area of a city or a village in some past time in the old, native country. The loneliness of the lost and the displaced; privileged, but displaced and lost.

So, unlike those with gypsy mentalities like my own, a restlessness where a steady job, a constant home, the daily routine of going to and coming from the same place, the endless repetition of the same faces in the same context, soon take on all the aspects of an imprisoned existence.

I thanked him again, and let him be. I had seen too much of this illness among the aged British in Portugal, who should never have left their soap opera lives at home for wild but silent dreams of paradise abroad that they should have had and should have pursued in their youth. They had not so much aged in life as aged in having missed it, totally, missed it as zooed animals miss life, miss their natural habitat where recognition, infallible recognition and instant, native reaction, of friend and enemy is of equal import, is all of life. Now they were too conditioned in routine habits to survive when released into their nature's element. The creaking cage doors finally opening to pensions and old age. And alcohol and sedatives; their day's highlight the late arrival of their favourite tabloid, their week's delight a soused bag of mangy — the way they really loved it, like — 'fish n chips, love'; the radios perpetually tuned to the BBC World Service. And they thought they had finally escaped the bloody farm ...

But I had nothing to do or think about. I wandered around. I expected some message, some signal, from even the most unexpected source; so strolling about aimlessly wasn't a good idea. I bought a local newspaper, picked out a sedate looking, respectable restaurant and entered. At the door a young man, maybe twenty, twenty-two, dressed in abysmal rags, was standing with his head bowed. When I entered the proprietor glanced at me for an instant then looked away, uninterested. I selected a table, sat down, ordered a glass of water and a coffee with a snip of lemon rind in it. The waitress smiled.

There was now another person standing at the entrance. She was a child of maybe fifteen, with little beauty, visibly under-fed and dressed in the same torn scarecrow clothing as the boy. A few minutes later a young business woman came in. She glanced at the proprietor as she entered and casually flicked a finger towards the boy. The proprietor nodded and spoke to the waitress. The business woman sat down and ordered coffee and a tuna salad with cucumber on brown bread. Perhaps this was power food. But Maria had said a diet of fresh fish, lightly fried, was a natural tranquilliser, if you ate pasta before it, or some garbage like that. I didn't remember. The woman looked self-assured, serene, with an easy competence and confidence in her world. It just crossed my mind I'd forgotten to take my sedatives again, today, and she had the kind of presence that could remind me of that.

The waitress scooped a mash of minced tuna and loaded the sandwich. Then she cut away the crusts from the bread and laid them on a paper napkin. She served the woman, then took the crusts out to the boy. He wolfed them, ignoring the girl standing next to him, and then remained standing there, his head still bowed.

Wait. That had not happened. I had dreamed that. That

could not have happened.

But the two of them were still standing there, heads bowed.

To test if I had gone mad, fallen into another world, I caught the waitress's attention, pointed at my coffee and mineral water and nodded towards the boy. As part of her job, without any hiatus of surprise, she poured the coffee into the water glass and brought the mixture out to the boy. He wolfed that too. In twenty minutes the boy was 'fed' and he left, leaving priority to the girl.

And so it went on; never more than two standing in the doorway, fed from the scraps the diners left behind. My realisation of the famine deep poverty so casually acceptable in an urban, a metropolitan, setting numbed me. Again and again I did not believe it. I had to watch, again and again, too dumbstruck to do anything constructive; to actually buy a full meal and send it out. When I did I made sure my bill was paid and I could leave quickly. And then, in leaving, I left in embarrassment, unable to meet the eyes of the recipients. Because they were recipients, not of my charity, but a tiny portion of my massive, collective guilt.

There was no one I knew in the Square. I bought a lemonade I didn't want — what was I supposed to do for Christsake? Moan about the umpteenth live demonstration in history of the free markets' inabilities to eliminate poverty and deprivation; to create the conditions whereby equality and justice must of themselves prevail? I should do this? Me? I who could not, to save my life, eat, literally, eat from another person's plate, must now be eating, gorging myself, in some way that still turns out to be literal, from the plates of more, many more, than one.

It is not the beggar who eats another person's crusts from another person's plate. The beggar eats his own crusts from his own upsurged plate, returned momentarily in an act that is all of guilt, but devoid of repentance, or even charity.

I sat in the shade. I missed her now, just where was she, my refuge in this world. I needed her. And I missed her, was bored with myself without her, felt bereaved.

And time wore slowly on. I noted the poor about the Square, the desperately poor, no, the famine stricken, stricken by an absolute lack of care, and literally starving, starving slowly, infinitesimally slowly, to death. And then I noted the innocently unseeing well dressed and well fed school children happily taking their midday break. What was their fate? And who cares?

Moments late, or some time later, the rainy season abruptly commenced. A deluge of water tumbling from the sky without warning, and I had to scamper for the shelter of the Central Bar.

I would otherwise have called them riffraff, the money-changers, the inept pimps, the lying salesmen, the petty thieves, the cunning little hoodlums, the worn out whores, the drunken seamen, the general clientele of this once historic hotel now gone to seed.

But I could no longer describe them so. I'm sorry to say it, but I saw their options in this goddamn humanly savage jungle, this humanly created jungle that makes nature's deepest cruelties squirm in revulsion, this goddamn modern failed God called the free-market, and I'm sorry to say that again, but I respected them. They were failures because they were normally human, because they lacked superhuman avarice, arrogance, and sadism. That is the true, exact word: sadism. Because they did not have the superhuman greed necessary to eat opulently and happily from the portions due to the plates of many, many others. That's why they weren't rich; it wasn't a lack of intelligence, stamina, a reluctance to work. Otherwise all the world would be rich. Even the lazy would work for riches.

When most I should have otherwise needed alcohol and sedatives I now could not abide the thought of either. I wanted to tear down the walls of this temple of Mammon humankind has built, a tiny proportion of humankind has built. It is not just Malthusianism that was ignored, or just Socialism that was rejected, or just Capitalism that has, yet again, failed. It is the human species. We have failed; we have already created our own doom.

We, the most communal of all the species, even more than ants, we who love to show off and swank to each other, amuse each other, dance with each other, dine together in good cheer and fellowship, love to revel in what the Irish call the craic; the unwounding but quick humour caught on the hoof in the chase of many subjects madly mingled into one communal conversation while we get pissed out of our trees with each other; need to look into each other's eyes and hold hands like children, need to tenderly touch and accept each other in all the huge, unclotheable, undisguisable, giantly trembling nakedness of our sexuality, and we strive instinctively to do this with love and delicacy. We, who even need enemies within our own species, we have created societies again and again that set us at each other's throats, smilingly at each other throats.

Marco Polo, the world's greatest ever merchant, said that in a merchant's world there is no more sane or sensible reason for doing anything other than a mercenary reason. He said this in the middle of what we benightedly call the Dark Ages.

And now we are back, to the last dark age, before our self-created extinction. We are as fucked up as that. Our entire species.

Yara came in, alone, and drenched.

'Where's Lia?'

'I don't know.'

'Don't fuck with me, Yara. Where's Lia?'

'She's got some private things to do. That's all.'

'Yara. Yara. I didn't ask the question you answered. I asked you: Where is Lia?'

'Please. Buy me a coffee.'

I did.

She whispered: 'Please promise me this: never hurt Lia. Please promise me this. I beg you to promise me this; I beg you never to hurt Lia in any way. We are not related, but she is the closest person in the world to me. And she is the only person in the world I have.'

'I swore to you before.' I showed her the flight tickets, the return flight tickets. 'And you never have to ask or implore or beg. I will never hurt her. I will never permit anyone anywhere to hurt her. And she is the only one I have in this world. Yara. We have a common interest, haven't we?'

'Yes. But let her tell you herself. Maybe she doesn't want to tell you, maybe she wouldn't want me to tell you because she wants to tell you herself. Yes. We have a common interest, haven't we?' And she smiled, almost like Ilana, a gentle, touché smile.

'I'm sorry, Yara. I'm in a lousy, lousy mood. I am disgusted.'

'I hadn't noticed.'

'Thanks.'

'Go to Maria's. She'll feed you pasta and fish and bananas and tell you stories and you'll just fall asleep.'

'You, Yara. You tell me a story. Any story.'

She shook her head. 'You remember you were eavesdropping and I told that awful story of having six guys in one night and all the other things? Well, I'm still alive because Lia objects to capital punishment.'

'That story, that story, did you read it somewhere?'

She was puzzled: 'No. Why?'

'You made it up?'

'You ought to know. It didn't fall out of the sky into my mind.' Her head shook lightly from side to side, 'Bits and pieces, my life, directly, indirectly. The other girls. Sex is so complex for me. I am so totally heterosexual. Yusmely ...' she shrugged. 'She doesn't know herself. But sometimes I want a guy to just put his arms around my bum and fuck me into the next world. Sometimes I don't like that at all. Sometimes if he does I don't like it, and if he doesn't I don't like it either. Shades and shades. Possession and independence and dependence. Independence of myself, possession of my body. Sometimes I'm confused. But I've had a lot of men, at least twelve. Different moods, mine and theirs. Sometimes it's just rutting, getting the kids for the next generation. I'd like kids. Sometimes I think they're more erotic than men, more responsive. Sometimes one man can feel like six hundred, but there's no sex, just weight and push and awkwardness and embarrassment. Some times I think I'll be celibate, and please myself. But that never lasts long ... It's not easy to tell stories about hedonism, is it? And that's sex, that's life.' Thus spoke Yara, who may have been quoting another book of the Apocrypha, deconstructed into a short story suitable for young ladies.

'Thanks for the stories, Yara. I needed that. Have you enough money for yourself, for today?'

'Oh yeah. The twelve dollars Sylvia paid for the English lesson; Lia gave it to me!' And she raised her clenched fists to her shoulders and shook them and went: 'Ah! Ah! Ah!' with the delight of triumph glowing all over her face.

Jesus, they ask for so little, and their lives are so abundant of life.

'I'm in Maria's if Lia comes in.'

'She won't come here.'

'Why not?'

'Who would, if they had a choice? Except this riffraff, and tourists. This life is the shortest, quickest way to boredom I've ever known. I didn't read that either. And I've read a lot.'

'You really feel that way? Bored?'

'Yes I do.'

'All the happiness, the smiles, the laughter?'

'So I'm a clown; I'm my own worst and favourite hypocrite. I read that somewhere.'

'Things will change, Yara. Things will change.'

'So Lia says, and every day I say the same. And every day, like today, I'm afraid they really will; and I won't know what to do.'

Maybe, this time, God, maybe just this one time, just once, you might think of giving them a break, this new generation. You might think about this, consider this: give them just one fucking break. This is a prayer.

'For one month, Yara, I can take care of you and Lia. One month. Guaranteed. I'll talk to Maria, and you can stay at the Napoli, and sleep safe.'

'Oh I can always do that,' she said, 'if I only had the courage.'

'Come. We'll go to Maria's now and fix it.'

'Oh no. I didn't mean that. But I'd like it. If you fixed it. Lia tried. But I didn't mean it that way.'

So I went out into the deluge. The Corkman was too miserable in his alcove to return my scowl. When he didn't I stopped to give him a dollar.

'I'm an educated man,' he said in plain English, and with the quite insufferable, educated-arrogance of his class. 'I have moral standards.'

'You mean sex?'

'Of course I mean sex,' he shouted. 'What guttersnipe school did you go to.'

This type is so prevalent, in every country, that I'm sure they do all go to the same school. They sneak around and about life with such vanity, and a total misunderstanding of self-respect. They are products, they are produced, they are all things of worth, of education, moral beliefs, political convictions, and they are never their own independent, reflective selves. Their self-assurance is always of a mesmerised fastness. It is easier to get through the eye of a needle than it is to get through to them. That is why they think they're God.

'Fish don't know that they are wet, Fella, a fish can't understand that it is wet. That's from Plato.'

It wasn't, of course, but his mouth opened in a droop; and that spoke more than all of Plato. That was the last time I ever spoke to him; the man who once was Irish, from Cork.

Lia wasn't at Maria's, and Lia wasn't with me, and immediately Maria was concerned, as concerned as I was, and
fussed. And blamed Yara.

There was also no message waiting for me. No one,
absolutely no one, had called for me.

I apologised for asking so persistently, but it was a bad
day for me. I told her the story of the famished poor
standing head bowed outside the restaurant and how this
touched something deeper than my understanding of
famine in a modern state, how it touched a humanity in me
I thought was already fully awakened, and had been fully
awake, for many years. She looked at me for a moment of
quizzical surprise. She was silent and bewildered. Then she
seemed to resolve the mystery by saying that proprietor
was the son of north Europeans, strict Christians, and he
believed the poor must suffer humiliation when they seek
charity. Otherwise they will never reform. He insisted they
stand at the entrance, to prove they were genuinely hungry
and not work-shy; unlike all the other places, from the Villa
Rica to here, the Napoli, where she saved the uneaten food
from the plates and handed it out to them, to the poor at the
back door.

'Here. You do that here?'

'Yes, the same as in Europe.'

It wasn't the same in Europe. But she said it was, when
she was a child there. And from the newspapers she read it
was worse there now than when she had left. Millions
living on public relief, they said.

But here, Maria, here, in the Hotel Napoli, did she give
leftover food to the poor at the back door?

'Yes,' she said, and seemed embarrassed, and looked for
something to do to avoid the conversation.

'But who would come here, Maria?'

'Well, people, just people,' she answered stupidly. But in

my dim mind a light began to flicker.

'What kind of people, Maria? Give me some examples.'

'Good people. Good, but poor people.' And she couldn't find anything to break my concentration on the subject. Perhaps she didn't, out of honesty, want to break it.

'I have been a mother, too,' she said. 'I know how hard it is for them when they're at an age. They make mistakes, let themselves down, and to admit it is to admit they're still children. It's not true, I know, but they think it is. And they are ashamed of their mistakes, and try to hide their shame. That's when they're being childish again. I told them. It was Yara who couldn't listen.'

I felt covered in shame. I tried hard, madly hard, to see the bravery, the gallantry, and to understand beyond reach, the extremity of the desperation.

'Is that how you first met Yara? And Lia?'

'Yes.'

'They were begging.'

'They weren't begging. They knocked on the back door. They asked for work. They were babies, then. Women, yes, young adults. Intelligent, a good education, better than I had at their age. But no information. They knew nothing real of this world. They were a little different, Yara and Lia, because they hadn't seen television, and had read a lot. They wouldn't tell me where they came from. They told me lies. And I pretended to believe them.'

'Lia stood outside the door and you passed out food to her?'

'No. I took them in. I took both of them in. I fed them and made them wash, they were stinking. I sent them to bed together. I thought they were sisters and anyway they were only children, then. They were so pious, can you believe that, so pious. They slept right through the day. And you know Lia screams and kicks in her sleep. I saw that. I watched over them as if they were my daughters. Thank God I only had boys. When they woke up I fed them again. I tried to make them feel at home. The rooms are mostly empty anyway. They were silly as girls and I would have let them both stay. They were starving in the morning and afraid of getting fat in the evening. I tried to help them. I told them things. They knew nothing. They had no information about the world, about this city, about life. Maybe Lia did, but she was very silent. I was more companionable with Yara. I warned them of Sylvia. I told them what Sylvia did. And I will never forgive Yara. She questioned me and questioned me and she was cheating me of my intentions. She wanted to go to Sylvia. She went that night. I will never forgive her. The first time she took a man she did it for money. She got twenty American dollars from Sylvia for it. She was a virgin. Maybe Sylvia got five hundred. He was a businessman and owned a restaurant in the city. What I am telling you is true. She came back the next morning with twenty dollars. As if it were a fortune. That's why Lia left; when I told Yara to leave. She had to keep up with Yara, to show she was as grown up a woman as Yara. I knew the pressure. But Yara went willingly to Sylvia.'

Maria seemed to have shrunk, in the way the dead shrink, some tiny, precious secret had escaped her, and she cried.

When I tried to comfort her she made herself rally and said she worried no more. Lia now had me, a serious man.

— Oh God, Maria —

I was lucky, yes, but Lia was very, very lucky. She had told her so, that she was very fortunate. And she didn't expect this nonsense of disappearing without telling anyone where she was going and she must be told again, firmly, when she returned, that she was not a girl anymore, but a serious woman, and must behave like one. I must tell her that, firmly, as a serious man.

I said yes, I would. I would speak to her.

But I was soaked with shame and humiliation. The last thing I would do was further abase, abash, belittle, Ilana, in any manner.

I was too numbed by the story to think anything but a million things all at once. And Maria stayed silent.

The jokes life plays on us, as if it were scripted.

It was as if I had lived all of Ilana's life in her body and her mind and had her raw pain inside me. And could smile, gallantly, like a cold sun turning warm as dawn breaks.

But who can undo the past? Who makes the present? What morality, what ethics, rule our species?

'It is better that Lia and Yara are apart.'

'There's no parting them, Maria.'

She did not answer.

I didn't want to part them anyway. I asked Maria. I said Yara had told me her behaviour was that of a clown, and she regretted her mistakes. I could vouch that that was true. I could vouch that she now understood the stupidity of what she had done. I could vouch that she now despised Sylvia. And she had asked me, she had said that she begged me, implored me, to assist her. And I had given her my word. So now I am asking, Maria, for charity, for mercy, to show mercy to me, and to permit Yara to return, and to stay. I am holding myself responsible for Yara's behaviour. I have already spoken to her seriously, as a man to a woman. Yara understands, now, how quickly life can turn to ruin; one silly, giggling, thoughtless step ... Her apprenticeship to life is over. She knows that now.

'May I bring her back, Maria?'

'Tomorrow night she'll be with Sylvia again!'

'Maria, I will not punish Yara. I will kill Sylvia. I will tell Sylvia Yara does not belong to her anymore.' Nor Judy, nor

Solange, none of them, but I did not say that to Maria.

'No you won't,' she said. 'You are too serious a man. I am an old Italian woman. That is passion talking. I can recognise that passion in a man, and I respect it. There will always be other Sylvias, always Yaras. Only God can now save Yara.'

'Where is your Italian heart, Maria? Where is your Italian heart? Let her back.'

She slowly raised herself and slowly started to walk around the dining table, slowly walked around that long dining table, looking at the floor, like, exactly like, an old woman wondering whether she should decide to live or decide to die. I think some women have this Brontë-like power in their minds.

'Bring her back,' she said.

I did, getting soaked again, and led a wet and a not particularly contrite Yara — who knew more about contrary old prudes, jealous bitches, than I ever did, even if I were a writer — back to the Hotel Napoli. I stayed around in case they should suddenly snap at each other. But Yara dried herself and set about being very serious, and sometimes even, sometimes, like a strictly obedient daughter. About to explode, at all the silly domestic chores Maria was making her do; making her do merely to disperse her embarrassed energies. Natural allies trying to remove a tiny bit of grit between them. There wasn't much conversation.

Finally, finally, Ilana arrived. There were just a few drops of rain on her smiling, relaxed face. She showed us her new ankle-length cape of clear, glistening plastic. Under that, she had a new, magnificent poncho, black, with sparkling gold lamé hems. She looked exquisite. And she was perfectly safe.

The relief of her arrival broke first ice between Maria and Yara, and while that was cracking, we left them alone and went upstairs together. Into our room, directly and immediately into our bed. And I wrapped my arms around her bottom, and. And whether this was a savage desperation of love, or whether this was a harsh rupturing of all my pent-up anxiety for her, or a perfect blend of my lust and love for her; or whether it was all poor Yara's fault, I'll never ever know. But she told me that she liked it, when she got her breath back. She said she sure wouldn't say no to that any night. And her smiles said more.

Then we went downstairs to eat. And I could assure Maria, by my face, that I was indeed a serious man, and Ilana was indeed an even more serious woman. And we were both in need of renewal, of sustenance, culinary sustenance.

So we ate much and talked a little, about international relations, the world economy, the stature of politicians, and movie stars; matters like that, the pertinent concerns of our gamekeepers.

With an ergodic quick-slow rhythm we became more sensible, and Yara complained that Maria had put too much butter in when the pasta was boiling. But Maria refused to quarrel, everyone to her taste, if she had any. Yara cleaned away the table with the confident bustle of a proprietress, and we settled to contentedly sitting about in each other's company.

No television, but I didn't want to strain Maria's already over taxed energy. The day wore down. Yara prepared herself for bed with some staggering comments to a bewildered Maria about the anti-ageing benefits of a life of celibacy. Ilana and I went to bed to age ourselves by yet one more day. And the mystery of suite 18 sent no message.

The next morning Ilana and Yara disappeared again, but with Maria's knowledge and consent. No one was going to tell me so I didn't bother to ask. I sat about reading *Praise of a Worthy Woman,* — by God, according to Maria, who now insisted that the dining-room, between meals, was my study. And she left me 'to mediate and to study and to compose.' This was a serious obligation, and I fretted under it all morning. That afternoon, taking the air between downpours, I found Papa.

He was a day old, maybe less, a tiny, miserable pup, too timid to whine, but trembling like a dog in the gutter of a street. This was on the corner of the Square Lisboa, beside the Carmo Convent, in the first days of the rainy season when the water fell, not like rain from the sky, but like a huge lake suddenly pouring itself out of the sky. The tropical sun and heat never ebbed, and an hour later all the buildings would be dry, all the street gullies swollen with muddish rivers of tumbling, dirty brown water.

I took Papa under the awning of a food kiosk and bought a hamburger. I fed bits to him, and he tried to eat. But this was more to please me and win my love than to assuage his appetite. I understood.

The massive rains stopped and the street kids, the beggars, the peddlars, and the dying, began to throng the Square with all the bustle of their lives. Papa was terrified. That was why I gave him the name Papa; to make him feel big and strong. Behind me, about five metres away, an old used-up woman of about forty had not broken her deathbed huddle on a stone bench during the downpour. It was nature's cruelty that she had not died yesterday. I gave her almost all of the hamburger that Papa couldn't eat. She smiled thankfully at me, and didn't speak, and quietly hid the hamburger under her body.

In the vicinity of the Square there were always two or

three people dying on the stone benches. They had no place else to go. You could see it in their eyes. I could see it in her eyes, then. Her only hope was to die easily, without too much pain although she knew there would be more pain. I could recognise it in her eyes. I did not know how to help. When everyone else walks past, and poverty and death are casual affairs of no note on the street, it is hard to know where to start. My own life was a fake. I had lost my life. My mind did what it cannot help doing in such circumstances, it blinked.

So I called the pup Papa; give him pride, a big, strong, sensible name: Papa. With a name like that you can walk like a king among dogs. I took this king back with me to the Hotel Napoli as a present for Ilana.

When she saw this added burden she smiled bravely and accepted it. Maria and Yara were out together, for Maria to verify something Yara had sworn was true. Maria was holding her strictly to it. So Papa was alone in Ilana's cuddling arms. The stupid pup thought he had it made. She gave him a small piece of bread and he refused it. I explained that Papa wasn't hungry; he had already turned down a full hamburger.

Where did I come from? she asked. Where cats were multilingual and always well dressed and even dogs were given such stupid, inappropriate names as Papa.

Well, more or less, Ilana, as an illustrative metaphor that had escaped me until now. But she was serious. She refused contact of any kind with the pup, and he tried to slink towards me. I shouted at him. He trembled back from me, and looked at her. But he could have been roasting in hell and she would have contentedly fed the coals. He looked indelibly sad, the indelible sadness in a dog's eyes, and still she refused him all contact.

He crawled across to the piece of bread and ate it, and

licked his lips, several times, and gazed beseechingly at her. She gave him one more piece, and he instantly swallowed it and gazed at her adoringly. And she turned, and smiled a strange smile to the wall, and turned back and buttered a piece of bread and fed it to him in her arms. It is not the first time in my life that I have been jealous of a dog, as an illustrative metaphor. But it passed my mind what similar tests she must have put me through, and how I was lucky enough to survive.

Maria arrived back alone, asking God to forgive her. She spoke with me, but was unhappy with me, was unhappy with herself. Then she was confederate with me, and still volunteered no information to me, but the world was strange, and you never knew the world.

Yara returned, with groceries, and the news that no one had seen Sylvia in two days, and no one knew where she was. Maria swung her head instantly to look at me, and of course it was impossible and she put the doubt away. Yara had proved something, and it had given her a new lightness and happiness in herself, and a new place in Maria's esteem.

Very thankfully, Papa was the centre of attention, they were even going to change his name, but Yara insisted it was too late; it would be traumatic for him, it could make him neurotic. I sat apart and fretted. That reality must come directly back into my life, at any moment. There was a randomness in the way I focused on my life. An irking, jumpy randomness. No alcohol, no sedatives, but I was increasingly conscious of myself and of taking myself, and other things, too seriously, one moment, inappropriately, and too casually and lightly, inappropriately, the next moment. I could almost feel the signal approach, and the selling, again, of my partially restored life. But it wasn't to come that night.

It came the next morning, when Ilana and Yara were out, and Maria was continuing to house-train Papa. Yusmely came shyly to the door and gave me the key to suite 18 and smiled, getting more and more bashful, and quickly turned away across the beam of her smile. I had to tell many lies to ward off Maria's aroused and snooping curiosity.

The rest was easy. I went to the Villa Rica, to suite 18. There was no one there and I could find no message, no instructions. On the desktop were Ilana's and my passports. Inside, the US visas were indented. I sat down and enjoyed the silent air-conditioning.

When he came in he had an attitude of casual benevolence and ease. There was nothing of the manner of an employer interviewing a prospective employee. There was more directness, of an individual wondering if he had found a colleague, a trustworthy colleague. And he wasn't armed, wasn't carrying a gun; didn't have a self-assurance of that kind. He spoke excellent English, studied and well-read, with a soft US accent. He commended me, first, on Ilana's beauty, and how lucky I was, but of course of more importance was her intelligence and character, which could only improve yet more with time.

He was indubitably calm, relaxed, and pleasant, about my age, and there was nothing whatsoever derivative in his manner or attitude other than an excellent education; a man who could pilot an aircraft and with equal competence discuss philosophy, and of equally wide personal experience, deeply reflected upon and studied. He was implacably impressive, and in no way showed any signs of being aware of that.

He sat in the armchair opposite me at the small, immaculately clean, glass table. There was no shortage of people with intelligence, and with good cover, like mine. The shortage was of people with characteristics they shouldn't have if they were doing this job: trustworthiness and character. Neither of mine had been proved, but there were signs. And describing Ilana as my daughter showed a nice touch, a nice lack of vanity. Unlike those who most often put themselves in the road for this line of work: executive boot-boys, executive skivvies, like Sylvia.

I was so glad he said that. It showed.

'But we do need such people,' he said, 'however personally distasteful they are.'

The last question was did I have the nerve, or did I need alcohol or sedatives? No.

Fine. Then I should re-book my tickets via Aruba. Money had already gone to the gold card account. If I dropped dead they could still use the card and recoup their investment. I knew if I accepted and then behaved negatively it would be suicidal. In Aruba I should stay at the Wilhemina V Hotel and open a bank account in each of the Island's banks. A key for a New Orleans accommodation address would be arranged. I should also tell people I was leaving a day earlier than intended. Then I should bring Ilana here and take the first flight the following morning. Of course, whatever baggage was here I would have to take with me.

No problem there, but Ilana had to be completely screened from this if anything went wrong.

'That can never be guaranteed,' he said. The authorities were so often morally corrupt. It was impossible to predict the course of their vengeance. But you could guess at it with reasonable accuracy in Ilana's case. I could either not take her with me, or, perhaps, from Aruba we could take separate flights.

It was a chance I had to take.

There were a dozen or more basic technicalities that had to be explained and understood. When this was done he asked if I agreed. I agreed. No qualms? No qualms.

I was eager to leave, there was much to prepare. But he offered me a coffee and was interested in anything I might say.

Particularly about my life. Yet if he had already known the gold card number I supposed he knew somewhat more. Reluctantly, and with extreme brevity I told him. Because Ilana had now, miraculously, changed the aspect, but not the reality, of my past. It was, now, the road to her. It now had that aspect. There was little time left to give her happiness, and no reasonable prospect of building a life together. There wasn't, simply, enough time. But I wanted as much abundance of happiness for her as possible.

Anyone of my age, dispossessed — of my life's reason, as I had been, — and displaced as I was, appreciated that the chances of a renewal of meaningful life were less than slight. Only a fool would fail to appreciate that any, any chance had to be immediately grasped.

I understood Sylvia's selfish, stupid, greedy misunderstanding of my needs, her implacable inability to see things other than through the distortions of her greed, and her misunderstanding of why I was carrying a gun the first night I met her, and of the terrible price she demanded for a passport; I understood that this was, finally, the price of my entrée to this chance. There had been no misunderstanding on my part.

He asked me to take another coffee and wait a reasonable time before leaving the suite. That was the first and only time I ever saw him.

No airport farewells; I cannot stand them. I had to stress this repeatedly to Maria and stridently to Yara. No airport farewells. So we took our holdalls in a taxi to the airport, and sat in the airport bar until nightfall, and then took a taxi to the Villa Rica. I asked for forbearance and forbearance and all would shortly be explained. But Ilana had already isolated herself in a tense alertness, and was more anxious to ask questions of prior, known reassurance rather than anxious to disturb the equilibrium she strove so hard, constantly, to maintain.

In suite 18 there was a fully packed suitcase of gent's clothes, most in drycleaners' wraps. There was also, inside a coloured plastic bag, an already sealed duty-free bag from Aruba Airport. It had two hundred cigarettes and a bottle of Scotch.

Ilana slept well in the cold of the silent air-conditioning, and for a while I thought her nightmare wouldn't visit, until it did, the most violent I had ever experienced.

Morning, and the flight to Aruba, and my surprise to find so many banks cluttered about the colonial main Square, and my amazement and amusement, and Ilana's disbelief, that so many banks were named with Irish surnames. Banks no one but the very, very rich had ever heard of. None of the locals on the island earned enough in a year to make even the opening minimum deposit.

We spent the night in the beautiful Wilhemina, even more opulent than the Villa Rica, and took the morning flight to New Orleans the next day. There was no way of leaving her alone, of being permitted to leave her alone, for any length of time. It was a very acute, deep, anxious worry to me for the time it took to get through immigration and customs, and no more. We took a taxi downtown. During the ride I scribbled some notes on a piece of paper. And each time I looked up Ilana thought I was looking for inspiration. I smiled. She smiled. The cabbie smiled, and said: 'Holy shit, you guys on your honeymoon?'

'Yes, well. In a way. I was occupied in the army when I shoulda been doing this.'

'Hey shit man they ain't never got me in no army. I been gettin' it regular since I was in short pants.' He laughed. I laughed too and asked if he was a typical New Orleanian?

'Born and raised.'

I tipped him, and he snapped his fingers at a bellboy. They exchanged some signals that I pretended not to see. I tipped the bellboy, too, and quietly asked him how one went about getting married in this town.

He said: 'Ah shit man!' and was well on his way to saying something about little South American beauties when he had a quick reappraisal of the situation as it pertained at that moment in time, and shut up. Then he told me of 'several possible scenarios', and went away chirpy and smiling.

Ilana was in a linguistic quarantine; understanding most of what I said, and not a word of the responses. But she was catching on with an excited quickness. So we rested in the room for an hour, and she drank a lot of water, very much like someone trying to surface into a new environment. Then we hired a car at the desk and drove around for a few minutes, to establish some nervous orientation, on the tourist-maps, of our locality in the city.

We put the car in the basement carpark, went upstairs, left the suitcase and the duty-free bag, took only our holdalls, and went back to the car. We drove to the accommodation address. I opened the box and put in the hotel's two electronic doorkeys, and withdrew an envelope exactly the same as the one I had first found under the garbage pail in the Villa Rica, the one with Ilana's passport. This had some instructions inside, but was otherwise quite packed with money. A lot of money in bills of all denominations. Money. In all the endless games of Monopoly with the aged Britons in Portugal I had never seen so much money. And this was real. US currency. Dollars. Money. We drove to the Merit Inn and booked a suite.

Amazingly, again, all we wanted to eat was pasta. The waiter in his presentation enticed us to try stuffed Mississippi catfish. So we ate it all, pasta, fish, and lobsters. We ate it all, and drank wine, on our private veranda overlooking the Mississippi river, wondering where the spirit of ole Huck might be wandering about out there on this the most signal night of our life together.

We were exalted. We felt exalted. In the huge, silent, rich ease of the hotel. The bliss. The sheer, rich blissfulness of it all. We could roll over in the exquisite sheets and chuckle. And rolled over again, and again. Laughing. And our world was chuckling with a baby's delight. Holy! Shit! Man!

So much change had come over both our lives so quickly. We were deliciously happy, in this huge bed, in the huge, private silence of the suite. Delirious. And then we had all this money. It was gluttonous happiness, and we wallowed in it, exaltedly.

Sleep was impossible. The phone menu in the dinette said push gate switch and make selection. So we selected pizza with garlic and olives, black, green, stuffed, with pineapple, and pushed in the numbers and waited, like errant children in disbelief. Maybe we had gone too far; maybe we could cancel all of this, abort the experiment, change channels, promise never to be bad again, to pray for forgiveness and be born again in Jesus. But we sat and waited in guilty anticipation. Then the phone rang, once. The window beside it sprung ajar. We opened it and there, inside, on an electronic successor to the dumbwaiter, was our pizza.

Hey Shit Man! It works! But this was greed, sheer greed, Sylvia's greed. Still, we took it back into the bedroom, opened a fresh bottle of wine, dismembered the pizza, and ate it.

The wine was finished and still no sleep within a million miles. To calm ourselves I tried to tell her of the mouse in Amsterdam. Waking up, after his catastrophe, rubble all around him, enraged cats everywhere with bared talons scratching madly at anything non-cat that moved. But he had become a mouse again, much older, poorer, and less wise, all his heart gone from him. He found a little hole in the rubble and hid.

But no, no; the story was finished. Even Yara couldn't understand it so far. And Yara was very good at parables.

'Is this what you talk about on your secret outings?'

'Sometimes.'

A little tiredness, a slackening of tension, blessedly, had come over her. A small shade of darkness was beginning to pucker around her eyes. She settled herself comfortably sitting up in the bed, the sheet tucked under her arms. Women of all nations, everywhere, do this; a genetic memory of Eve. And then they shake out their hair.

'This is paradise,' she said, very simply, 'this is heaven,' and reached to take my hands in hers. Then for no reason she snatched away one hand to wipe away a tear for which there was no reason. And put the hand back in mine and began to cry.

For a long while she simply kneaded my fingers, and sat watching her hands squeezing and caressing, tightening and loosening.

She wasn't a German, she said. Papa had been a German immigrant, an electrician, but he disappeared — no, not that way, ran away — when she was five or six. Mama was Brazilian all the way back to Pedro Alvares Cabral. And

Mama had left five or six years ago. Papa gone, and you had someone to comfort you, and sweets and indulgences and hugs and it soon got endurable, despite the long sadness each night of going to bed without a story from Papa. But Mama leaving, that was impossible, that was the strangest experience, coming home from a long and bitter school day, and finding someone else living in your miserable apartment. And the neighbours saying your Mama didn't take you with her in the bus? Maybe she only forgot — Run after her, quick. And the callow giggles from inside, and it seems that there are sniggers everywhere and you are all alone on the street, penniless and hungry and twelve years old. Too numbed to be frightened, too frightened to be numbed. Bewildered. In a whole world that has suddenly materialised before you, and is full of nothing but danger and alarm. Street children are not brought by the stork. You become very holy to yourself, very far inside. And secretly eke out miserable resources as if they were great pleasures. With a lack of sensation in your mind, like after a heavy blow, that all your trust is gone from you, forever. You know the streets? You've lived on the streets? How closed and hard a thing a city is.

Processions of doorways that you may not enter. There is no doorway you may enter. Because Mama found someone to take care of her, and I was a complication. The others on the street had been at least a day longer on the streets, and were wise and selfish and cunning and laughing at my innocent mistakes. Because I could not truly believe that this was the truth of my condition in the world. I had no world.

In the church that evening, because I had nowhere else to go, they were singing songs of praise for the fall of Communism, and warning of its resurrection. The missionary priest spoke beautiful Portuguese, elegant,

schooled Portuguese, asking the Communists to come
home to Christ, now, the Eternal Father would understand
and forgive: 'What gain hath the worker from his toil?'
These were the words of God. Come back to God, he
begged the Communists, he said. Come back to your
spiritual home. Come back to Christ.

She stopped. Her hands were limp in mine and her face
was turned to sorrow, this the very most beautiful face of
sorrow. Beautiful in its sorrow, and it was all of sorrow.

'Hug me,' she asked, and I did. 'Hard,' she said. 'Harder.
Harder.' And she at once fell into sleep in my arms.

She slept reasonably well that night, despite another
brief, violent nightmare; and whenever I looked at her in
her sleep she looked content and happy in her gentle
quietude.

When I saw the sun rise over the Mississippi Delta I
assumed I must have slept. But it didn't feel like it. I lay and
told myself the continuation of the story of the mouse in
Amsterdam.

When she awoke, hours later, she at once, naked, walked all over the suite, bedroom, dayroom, office, shower and toilet, dinette, the verandah, even the verandah, and stood naked to my terror and surveyed the Mississippi. She came back, smiling; the known world hadn't vanished overnight.

We showered and didn't eat, because we were going to have to eat a lot of garbage that day. Now it was time to work, again. Opening chequeing accounts, at banks, credit unions, saving and loan societies, meekly lodging in each, again and again, all we had brought with us from Ireland to the new world.

'Would you like a secured credit card with your checking account, Sir?'

'Yes, thank you.'

'That's five dollars, Sir.'

'Just one, please. She's old Irish and only speaks Irish. So one will be enough until she learns American. She's learning how to speak American now.'

'Gee, that's cute.'

If only you knew, lady, if only you knew.

Because there are no hyphenated Brazilians. But all over the US there are hyphenated Americans, so many of them telling me they were Irish-Americans. Making me think of the jerk who once originally was Irish, from Cork. This is part of their amnesia-screen. When truly exasperated by this I used to explain that they hadn't killed Geronimo. As a matter of fact, pal, he had escaped to Ireland and married my grandmother, a Belfast Presbyterian. Hence my children would be Irish-American Irish-Indians, and practising Presbyterians. Better circle the wagons again. Or any such exasperated lie that occurred to me.

Yet there were those who always touched my heart. They started out in full Americana accents and after a few drinks dehydrated an odd syllable, more and more frequently, you could hear the accent of Kerry, or Yorkshire, or Hamburg or Sicily or wherever breaking through. With these I always feel a companionship, a sense of community. Because I am aware the Irish, and the British, have amnesia-screens, too.

We spent all that money opening accounts. There was more, always, at the accommodation address. When there wasn't we cruised from fast-food joint to fast-food joint, sometimes having to eat, sometimes messing up a prospect. Then we found one. A sophomore called Linda, pinned to her uniform. Bright, vivacious, and as gullible as a hamburger.

'Hiya, Linda.'

'Hiya, what can I get you folks?'

'Hey! I can see you reading my mind. Two big Macs with fries. Two medium coffees, black. Bet you knew that.'

'Sure did.'

'Yep. Can always tell a Sagittarius.'

'Hell no I'm a Gemini. See my bracelet. My boyfriend bought me that.'

'No way. You're not scatter brained, indecisive, unfulfilled. You're a Sagittarius. I'm really into it. I can tell.'

A little vibrancy gone from the bounce.

'Guess you got it wrong. I'm a definite Gemini.'

'No way.'

'Six ten seventy-four. That's me.'

'I'm just making a big mistake here. I should have guessed. The Gemini is complex, intuitive, sensitive to change. I got it. Hell what was I thinking of. You're outa state, ain't that it?'

'Wrong again.' But bounce restored.

'Got it. Bet it's double Gemini. Let me guess. Yeah, bet your Mom is Gemini, of Irish extraction, you with me? and her name is. Wait. Houligane? Right?'

'Shit no. That's my Dad. He's James Ireland. That's his

exact same name.'

Prospectors in the Klondike used to get a buzz like this when they hit a vein.

'But Mom's from Baltimore. Cassidy, reckon that's Italian, don't you.'

'Sure is. Maria Cassidy. Sure is.'

'No she's Joan.'

'Well, goddamn. This is real double Gemini stuff. Complex, incisive, quick, intuitive pattern solving. Bet you don't fit into crowds easy? But I just love that IQ.'

'Bet you got me figured for a college student, right?'

Manifest belief: 'Right!'

'Well I am too. But you sure didn't know it!'

'Knew you were going to say that, Linda. Can't beat an education. Where's the smoking area? Me? Yeah, I'm Sagittarius, anxious to please, humorous, easy to get along with, dumb as shit. Way over there? Right. And you too. Have a nice day. And watch out for your head. Bet all the boys just love it, hahaha.'

She just ain't never gonna tell Pop about this.

Just hold, Ilana. Eat this culinary junk like you enjoy it. They charge twenty five cents for a glass of water and give you gold for nothing.

But she did, anyway, like the muck, and ate like she was starved.

Canal street, and the Town Hall. For me the pre-Computer Age application, with the details I'd written down from the cabdriver's ID sheet; for Ilana the Computer Age application for the birth certificate of Linda Ireland. Clerks too accustomed to people who don't know a damn thing about themselves, bureaucratically speaking. Figuratively speaking, nonfiguratively speaking. Wait: five minutes. Certificates, ten dollars.

Upstairs, more application forms. Street, photographs.

Police station. Please authenticate these photos for our
Driver's Permits. More lies, and the unfailing respect of a
real dumb citizen. Thank you, Sir. Complete application,
some inventiveness, sign, wrap everything up, hand the lot
back in.

Ten days, Ilana, we'll have US passports waiting at our
accommodation box in the wall. Or the FBI. No, the FBI has
nothing to do with Ireland. One step at a time, child, the
twelve glorious steps to American citizenship, disenfranch-
ising someone else. The original, manifest American way.
Only dumb jackals prowl around cemeteries.

'Why didn't you do this in Brazil?' she asked.

'Because I didn't know then. And it would have been a
mistake. A wrong signal.'

But just one more rushing bout of panic for you, dear
Ilana.

Anxiety like wild-fire in her eyes.

Your national ability. No problem.

But the telephone book was a problem. Then under
permits, we found the driving schools and Our Lady of the
Assumption. We needed an instructor of the Latin
community. He knew the rules of the road computer test off
by heart and first coached her in passing that. Then three
hours in the driving lot, forwards, reversing around poles,
parking on a ramp, reversing up a ramp and parking. Then
an hour on the road, with her incredible equanimity and
gentle gallantry, and finally the test centre and a Brazilian
waltz through the examination. A nice, shining Driver's
Permit.

Check the accommodation address again. More money.

Back to the Merit Inn: 'We are pleased to announce only
Gold Card Guests are invited.'

Back in our huge suite; to laugh out loud, and scamper
and romp in our private, secret world. And relax, dine in,

and let this luxury pamper us some more.

Take a swim, 'Linda'. Practise your English. You know it. Be brave.

In the foyer, an elderly American gentleman, wearing light tweeds in this magnificent, tropical city. Ilana, a face of budding innocence, gallantry overpowering timidity.

'Hey shit man where ist the pool, please, Sir?'

Cardiac arrest imminent on the old boy's face. But a dash of youth coming smilingly back into his eyes.

We found the pool for ourselves, remembered we weren't in Brazil, and hired a set of togs.

Back to our suite, refreshed, to laze about, and fall asleep at any old time.

That night her nightmare was very mild. It's blasphemous, I suppose, to expect miracles to be quick.

The next morning she drove me from place to place. I collected the cheque books and the credit cards, and deposited a few grand extra at each place — because, lady, we now realise a credit card is safer.

At the end we had enough credit cards, almost, to form a deck of playing cards. Then the drudgery of signing the first three cheques in each book, and dropping all but the credit cards back into the mailbox.

Another swim. Showered. Groomed. The marriage permit; and the drive to Our Lady of the Assumption Church on the banks of the Mississippi river. There, the Rev. Ramirez, Archbishop of the First Free United Catholic Church of the Parish of Louisiana, prepared to join us together in the bond of holy wedlock. His English wasn't even as good as Ilana's, and he intoned it as if we were about to be clapped into irons together in some religious dungeon.

And hence: the ceremony.

I thought it was all she wanted. Not all, as a state of being, but as the statement missing in our relationship, a public, official declaration that I would always love, honour, and cherish her.

There was even a hint of tears, and I knew she missed Yara. But she smiled bravely, and radiantly.

Silently, alone, we drove back to our hotel.

I told her she had just made me a king among men. She smiled and rallied. We ordered champagne, via the dinette-phone. And pasta, out of deference to Maria's spiritual presence. And then we ate our marriage dinner alone. I ordered gin, and we mixed it with the champagne.

It puzzled me, and I realised how little I knew her, when she insisted, wifely, that we consummate 'our nuptials'. And she strove mightily, with a gentle, persistent mightiness, to show me how serious a duty this was to her.

She succeeded, and for the first time in my life I was, immediately thereafter, serious in a way I had never been before, in a way I could never have been before. Perhaps Maria had always known the future.

When she slept it was the first normal siesta time sleep during which her nightmare, and most viciously and brutally, came to her. The first time ever. Holding her, just holding her rebelliously berserk body, and trying to calm her, exhausted me. When some peace came to her, and she lay quietly, I went fast asleep.

When I awoke she was sitting in an armchair at my side of the bed, the polaroid photographs of the wedding torn into scraps at her feet. Her face was expressionless, and she did not answer me. I thought it was an honest, abrupt, unfearful rejection of all, and silently went and showered. I stayed a long time in the shower, letting the water spray hard on my back. I turned it to cold and made myself endure it. It hurt. The water sprayed its ice coldness into every pore, and my breath heaved. For a moment I thought: if only I could cry, if only I could suffer my pain, and my many impossible fears, in my sleep.

Her hands touched me, she brushed aside my fright and my arms and hugged me, instantly very close and fast to her. Conflicting priorities and I tried to turn the gauge to warm and she laughed against her tears and said she didn't mind. I promised I would marry her again, in Brazil, in a proper church, with flowers and tiers of wedding cake, and Yara and Maria and her friends and guests, and confetti and bridesmaids and a guard of honour made up of real Archbishops and Cardinals. She grinned, like a child missing a front tooth, and promptly slapped my buttocks as if I were an impossible child. Then she became amorous to me, sharply, a tilt in her stance, her arms promptly around my shoulders, her mouth sucking on mine, and her native tongue speaking an ancient language in my mouth. A fluency of tenderness and love, a vow of fealty no pope or king or president ever received. A vow filled, fulfilled, in its giving. When she dressed, in goddamn denim jeans as if she didn't know skirts existed, she also wore that magnificent svelte black poncho with the gold lamé hems. I told her it was fetching, chic, racy, but tomorrow we were going to shop, shop for clothes. She looked at me like the Kerry cat watching the foil peel off a tin of sardines.

We rode downtown in a cab, because tonight we were going to drink champagne and gin, a lot of gin and champagne. At the corner of Bourbon Street we tipped off the cabbie and strolled down to the Ole Absinthe Pub, the birthplace of jazz. But the champagne wasn't good and the music wasn't live so we left. Perhaps this square mile is the most civilised place on the face of this planet, and we strolled lazily about in its atmosphere, and here and there refreshed ourselves with gin and champagne.

It was, perhaps, the fourth bar we entered. It was relaxed and disorganised and pleasant, and the activity was that of an intermission. The walls were hung with portraits of great American writers from Cooper, Hawthorne, Melville, Thoreau, perhaps the entire canon, to Steinbeck, Kerouac, and Faulkner. There was one portrait veiled. The bar settled, not even half full, and a young woman began to sing, acappella, Bessie Smith's 'Young Woman Blues'. When she was finished an old, nervous man, made an almost inaudible, shy speech, reading from notes, and got some shouts of Hallelujah from the quiet, anxious audience. Then the old man unveiled the portrait of James Baldwin and the girl began to sing: 'Tell Me How Long The Train's Been Gone'.

The bar shook with a joyous, ceaseless applause, and a breathless sense of relief, fulfilment. We were, all of us, publicly, in the middle of our private ceremony of remembrance, of joy and rage, grief and atonement, sacred, profane joy, profane, sacred rage, honour and shame, praise and gratitude, in all of which we all partook, body and soul, the empathy and the epiphany, to the life of a man who had been to us our voice, black and white, the dispossessed, our voice and rage and pain made articulate and elegant and, almost, effective.

The girl finished, but the atmosphere raged; the story of all our lives: Tell Me How Long My Train's Been Gone.

The girl swayed, and crooned, broken mumblings of words, the language of pain. She was stoned, sleepily and carelessly stoned, her voice formed by her sadness, and she began another song:

> *When the train left the station*
> *It had two lights on behind*
> *The blue one was my blues*
> *And the red light was my mind.*

For all the huge suites of luxury in my life, I felt forlorn. Here, next to Ilana's solid, immeasurable love and trust, I felt a part of me forever forlorn, felt that an essential human part of me had died long ago, had never known rest or comfort, never fulfilment. How ancient and how primitive the contemporary world seemed to me.

Oh Ilana, if you had known me twenty years ago. Then you would have been proud of me.

She didn't understand; she said she was very proud of me. Anyway she hadn't been born twenty years ago. But she knew from a little experience, and from Yara, that the young men were mostly callow, and often harsh and brutal and selfish. And as vain as little girls. She snuggled next to me, happily, and we both rallied. And bought some more champagne. Neither of us found it an acquired taste, but natural. And with a kick of gin.

Our night ended towards dawn as we sat on our verandah, and watched the sun rise safely on another day.

We slept late into the afternoon, and most definitely she slept soundly and untroubled.

We went to 'La Galleria' shopping mall. Forty-eight shoe shops alone, innumerable others of all descriptions. But even in this sanctuary of riches there were the ominous gun-shops. Fifty dollars down and interest free credit with monthly repayments of your convenience, and you could walk out with an automatic machine pistol, or one, or several, from a deadly selection of other instruments of war. Here, where a gram of cocaine earned a ten-year prison sentence, you could buy, for your own use, sport and protection, an instrument that could kill a hundred people a minute. And will be just as potent a hundred years from now. I asked about explosives, but a permit was needed; though the saleslady explained I could buy as many bullets as I wished and split the explosive out from the full metal jackets. Ilana was threatening outraged rebellion, thankfully, so I smiled in a henpecked way, excused myself, and left.

I was happier being asked my opinion on bras, panties, blouses, and skirts, and even the goddamn all stretch, pre-used looking, denim jeans she insisted on buying — they lift and pout madam's bottom, the saleslady said to her, as if nature had not already done this for Madam's bottom, to my provocation. I bought my y-fronts, socks and teeshirts in pre-packed delicacy, got measured for a few pairs of slacks, and swore to the immigrant tailor I'd visit the gun-shop if he attempted to pout my buttocks. But he was already on my side, and expertly fitted me out, with a few matching shirts and jackets, as if I were a gentleman.

At the accommodation address there was money and travelling instructions. Las Vegas. But first back to 'La Galleria' and its umpteen jewellers, and gold Cartier and Rolex watches, ladies and gents, in each, and gold wedding bands, matching gold necklaces, bracelets. Jeweller after jeweller. Cash; old country habits, Sir. And another

shopping mall, and more and more and more. The solid
leather portmanteau we filled with gold items was
crammed when we left it in the safe care of the Merit. We
checked out and flew to Las Vegas that night, our check-in
to the sister hotel prearranged by courtesy-management.

A limousine met us at the airport, the driver sitting so far
away from us that conversation was impossible. Then the
casino, where customers often lose fifty grand a night, and
come back, night after night. Wandering around playing
games we didn't understand. Then cashing in the chips we
bought for cash that disappeared down the tubes to the
fortified vaults below, in exchange for impeccable, certified
cheques. The wash cost less than a thousand dollars, and
was fun.

Next morning, another accommodation address, money,
another round of banks, same lies, same success.
Information from casually met Lindas and cabdrivers and
two more applications for two more passports. Shopping
malls and more gold. Evening, and more dallying with
gambling chips for an hour or two before exchanging them
for cheques. Then another casino, and another. Bed just
before dawn. Ten days, and back to New Orleans for a
twenty-four hour break.

Then Miami, more banks, more lies, more casinos, more
gold. And this time cars; secondhand cars. Two from each
lot. Drive and park in a dockside warehouse. Again and
again, leaving a portmanteau of gold watches and chains
haphazardly in any trunk. Keys and papers into
accommodation address. Until our new US passports were
forwarded from New Orleans and Las Vegas and it was
time to go to Jacksonville for a quick visit to the Greyhound
Bus depot. The manifest hunger of the people in this
locality, as it seemed everywhere except in the environs of
the Merit and La Galleria, physical hunger, emotional,

psychic hunger, their obvious consciousness of being excluded from the dream, of being undervalued and demeaned, and their razor sharp resentment. A very quick visit to the restroom. There, a rapid dispensation of the gold cards, the old passports, and numerous credit cards about the stalls. Out. And there we disappeared, bureaucratically speaking, from the face of the earth. Here, the posse just gonna have to split up into at least three different directions, and spend their lives crisscrossing the various trails in a rigmarole that won't end until the expiry dates expire.

Back to Miami, hence New Orleans, to Baton Rouge. Work on the new passports. Cheap studio apartment. Phone, cheap clothes on convenient repayments, cheap watch, ditto, cheap appliances from utility companies. All paid off in cash the next week. So the central computers sent their programs to the nearest roundabout to dance a jig of delight and frustration. Some people actually manage to pay off their debts, before they die. Some, just some. Three percent of the US population, as a matter of fact.

Otherwise triple A credit ratings awarded. Automatically, offers of gold cards flow in. Thank you. And while the pre-owned US cars were being shipped south where their cargo of gold would be discreetly removed and the cars sold for ten times their US price, but in local currencies, Linda and I flew to London, and another ten million US dollars had been cleaned and pressed as spanking new as school children and were respectfully travelling to their idyllic and sedately tropical home in Aruba.

London was superb, but a tiresome city to work in. Too many primitive gear-shift cars clogging the roads, motorised tin cans, and driving a competitive, macho activity. But the banks were plentiful, with well behaved, polite staff terrified of losing their jobs. And their little warrens of bedsitters.

Then Dublin, for a holiday. And perhaps her anticipation to see this city would turn to love and she would want to stay. How I would face that dilemma I did not know. But there was so little Irish beauty and grace to be seen on the faces of the people; it was there, yes, but rarely, very rarely, and dimly flickering, not ablaze, so little natural pride, the pride of waltzing Matilda from those who were cousin to the hundreds of thousands who had been transported as if they were dumb beasts to the other end of the globe, and who had survived and triumphed, and without bitterness; and so much assertive, brutal arrogance, a callow technique for want of style; as if the population had been culled of its young, its natural beauty, its talent. An entire generation seemed to be missing, as if it had just disappeared.

There was nothing of the spirit of O'Leary and O'Higgins, as if all the statues in all the South American cities were concrete lies, nothing of the Irish myths one hears everywhere in the world. Not a trace. As if it had been culled and dispersed about the world.

The streets were full of the old and infirm dragging themselves about without the aid they needed, full of the vacant expressions of the poor and unemployed, and of a class that had the rough attitude of garrison ghets from designer areas of penitentiary, oppressive slums all over the city. And everywhere, everywhere, the immense numbers of the remnant Irish left behind; the halt, the lame, the infirm, the abused, mentally and physically, everywhere in the midday drizzle under the lowered skies; and the crying and crying and crying of the children, the wards of deformed personalities moulding others to their own image and likeness.

Perhaps she'd like to see Kerry? It was different, very

different. Maybe the cat was still alive, wandering in furcoated luxury about the mountains, without a gold card. We were standing in the main street of this inner city in its slow, terminal despair.

No, she said immediately, let's get out. Let's get out today.

In Frankfurt, in Berlin, in Hamburg, the people were better dressed, and we even met some Irish whom she could recognise, Irish of beauty and talent, but there also there was no notion of community, of compassion and informal respect and dignity in the daily exchanges of human intercourse. But the banks loved cash. How deeply they loved cash. Then Lisbon, and the joy of Latin culture and attitudes. We wrote Maria and Yara that we'd soon be home. But we dallied in this crowded beautiful city. Then we flew to Recife, long after another ten million had gone sparkling home to Aruba.

In the wrong area of the city she showed me the place where the missionary priest had brought her on the evening of the day her mother had left her. A group of semi-renovated slum houses run by Womankind Worldwide to save the children on the streets. But it was not the place for her. She stayed a little while, until the priest found another place for her.

We asked some questions, got some information. We drove to a nearby church, asked, paid a donation, and got a real, true baptismal certificate for Ilana, and a lot of its information she immediately treasured.

We drove around again, while she watched for landmarks, here and there, and finally found the street, found the house. She left the car, to the gawping curiosity of many curious and happy children playing about in the dirt of the road. She left the car and went slowly, timidly, to the wall of the house. For a quick, brief moment she placed the open palm of her hand against the wall, and bowed her head. I couldn't remember where I'd seen that gesture before. But for that moment, for that fractional moment, the street went silent, the universe was silent. Then she got back into the car, her eyes and expression lost in the past. I encouraged her to cry, but it was not that kind of sadness. The emotions were still too stunned to gain such precious freedom. I knew when she wanted a conversation, an episode, to end, and when she didn't need questioning. In silence we returned to the most speakable, tranquillising luxury of the local Villa Merit Hotel.

Then we went home, to a glorious welcome from Maria and Yara, the dining room walls a shrine of postcards from exotic places with fabulous names.

We celebrated. For days we celebrated. Life became a celebration of each day, each night. This was a time to cherish.

We were well established in settled lives of ease and opulence. But it was hard to tell. Ilana and Yara disappeared each morning for hours at a time, sometimes with Maria, and always with Papa in tow. They were happy. They found busyness and things to do everywhere. My days began to be more and more emptied of activity. I wandered aimlessly around. I flew to Belem and came back with a suitcase full of books. Still, time was limp on my hands.

Other matters had been arranged. For the price of just about two plain, run-of-the-mill Rolexes we bought the Hotel Napoli from Maria. It was Ilana's property. Maria a perpetual, rent-free tenant, and now with a lot of money in the bank. Ilana made some arrangement with Yara. She didn't tell me, naturally, but I sensed it. It was taking time to get their genuine passports from the government, and some people were being stupidly greedy. I left a message about this at the Villa Rica, and the process speeded up. The courtesy also improved. But I was bored. They were happy. They always had pressing priorities to take care of. And I had no reason at all not to be happy, supremely happy.

Meandering across the Square I met Sylvia and Yusmely, and nodded hello, and wanted to walk on. Sylvia reminded me I owed her a thousand dollars.

'Go fuck yourself, Sylvia.'

'I'll fix you,' she said. 'I'll see to it.'

From that brainless, greedy, vain, assertive, selfish bitch this threat was unacceptable. When she saw my eyes again she knew it too. But she was too dumb to know it was already too late. I left a note about this threat to my security at the Villa Rica and Sylvia was not seen again.

But I didn't know that, then. Yusmely, coming up to speed, enticed me to decipher the words of Waltzing Matilda, another song she had spent a fortune on learning off by heart from the jukebox. I sat in her lovely company on a stone bench in the Square; and we got it right. All of it. We really worked on it until we got it all right. I could hear an almost native fluency in this language start to form on her tongue. She was delighted. She shook my hand and dared to quickly kiss me on the cheek before scuttling away. And minutes later scuttled back with a string of kiosk-photos of herself — her present to me, to remember her by. I understood.

I meandered back aimlessly to the Hotel Napoli. Time wore happily on, leading nowhere. It was this aimlessness, this lack of a goal, that irked me. The night when Yusmely knocked on the door and slipped the key of suite 18 into my hand I became exhilarated. I was at once refreshed and animated. I went and read the instructions. Another trip, more or less the same as before.

But Ilana was astonished, blankly astonished. She refused to go. There was no question of it. No. And had I forgotten my promise to marry her again, here, in Brazil. Endless formalities, questions of my citizenship. But OK. When we came back. We could find some priest who needed the money and understood a little of life's complexities.

She was very angry. I saw the anger turn to quiet rage. I changed. I asked her permission to go, and she refused it. I had no choice. I had to go. There were imperatives to be recognised. Yes, she could agree to that. But she was not going. She would never leave Brazil again.

Merely for something to say, something to ease the tension, I said perhaps it would be a kindness to take Yusmely with me. She could stay in the US. She longed for that with all her heart, to live in the US.

Ilana stood frozen. Under no circumstances. If I must go I must go alone and remain faithful. No, absolutely no further talk of Yusmely.

It was amazing, how little compassion she had for a fellow sister. She even called her bitch.

This was silly, bitter nonsense. I loved Ilana, only Ilana, look at the now permanent marks on my arms. I never pried, I never asked; I respected her freedom, I wanted her to tell me only what she herself wanted to tell me. But that would never be the limit of what I should know, or assume, or believe. There was great danger there, and she must know that. And now she was jealous of a girl who had nothing and no one in this world. It was preposterous.

Ask me, ask me, ask me, she said. Everything in my life, from the day we came here, together, for the first time, and you told me to undress and go to bed properly, everything in my life before that day is fictional. Fictional. Make-believe in my head. And now it is dead. For me it has all died. When I touched the house in Recife it was to touch the grave of my childhood, to say goodbye. My life became real, I saw your life become real, when we came together. So I have Yara and Maria. OK. For ten days, or fourteen, or thirty, but no more. Thirty days. You can go. But you must be faithful. And you must come back to me.

I promised. And I meant it, then.

We were so close that it is incorrect to call our exchange a disagreement. It was just a rapid exchange of information, and of the heat associated with that rapidity. Immediately afterwards she was of full assistance to me.

It was prudent to assume that the mad fanatics of the modern Inquisition against heretical forms of intoxication ran routine checks, that perhaps they maintained paid informers. On a randomly chosen night we went to the Villa Rica, collected the suitcase and the duty-free bag and flew to Recife. We bought a similar but not identical suitcase, packed it with male and female clothing and booked two tickets to Dublin via London. We checked in, Ilana checking in my case on her ticket. When the flight was called Ilana went to the toilets, swallowed half a pat of soap, became violently ill, and missed the flight. She said she had let the ticket fall into the toilet bowl when the fit of vomiting overcame her. Fear of flying, they said. Everyone gets it sometimes; don't let it worry you, you'll get over it too; we'll put you on the next flight. But no, no, she demanded her money back.

Before they got through dealing with this headstrong young woman I was in Dublin airport watching the two suitcases on the luggage carousel, and selected the proper one. If stopped I had just mistaken it for mine. The baggage stub wouldn't match. Then I flew back to London and hence to Miami.

The same tricks again. Variations on a lie; the basic lie of bureaucratic identity. But I missed her. Not having her presence near turned the aspect of the world to a very rotten colour. Many times, while being patronised by some official or clerk whom I was suckering with hillbilly innocence, stupidity, and earnest sincerity, I found myself examining the peasant, actually watching the neanderthal characteristics. How identical he was to himself six thousand years ago; so utterly and naturally *au fait* with his surroundings, so sure he was alive in enlightened times, so handily and cleverly making out, realising his potential, clicking the flint against the stone with the panache of a born survivor, a leader of men, pecking at the digits of a mobile phone, with the proud imbecility of a monkey tapping at a coconut and holding it, enchanted, to his ear. I have had more credit cards than most Indians have ever had arrows, of all patterns and colours and varying arcs of utility. But to watch these jerks use them was to watch a caveman display his most primitively coloured bow and arrow for the envious delight of his contemporary and identical idiots. To ask him to understand he was doing what he'd been farmed to do, and doing it poorly, was to expect the ass to break into heavy conversation well streaked with illuminating flashes of wit.

I was tooling around MacArthur Avenue, going towards Fisher Island terminal. Slip roads to shopping malls appeared and disappeared like exits into other worlds. The Southshore advertised itself as the world's largest mall, eighteen mile long, beach-fronted, six levels, forty restaurants. Whow! Man!

There was so much I couldn't do because she wasn't with me, and therefore so much aimless time on my hands. About the streets was the usual collection of the ill, of beggars, derelicts, the homeless, the alcoholic, the drop-outs. And there were so many of all of them. So many. An excellent source for passports. Try it?

I stopped off. A dollar, kindness and compassion, a coffee, ten dollars, and they told you their great grandmothers' maiden names and dates of birth, their useless 'Social Security' numbers, and most pretty quickly figured there was an angle, but weren't patriotic, and with Neighbourhood Watch they were not friends. They just upped the price. You could tell, very easily, those who were lying or didn't really know, and those who did and didn't care. Just so long as you valued it with money.

Drop me into the shit on this man and I'll come back and blow your fucking head off. You understand me, my friend?

Ain't goin nowhere.

Don't, and I'll come back and give you another hundred.

I'll talk to the fellas, get that kind of information easy.

Nice bait, my friend. I appreciate what you're saying.

Hundred a go?

Right.

See ya.

See ya.

I went into the world's largest emporium of consumerism. Sprinkled with drop-outs who hadn't quite hit the ground, yet. They are just a little different from the poor and huddled masses yearning to get off the soup lines and the sidewalks in all the US cities. The drop-outs are younger, and still remember the time when they dreamed of making it. They come pre-starved and pre-frightened, ready for instant co-operation; willing, anxious, to sell their adolescence, their adulthood, anything, for an in to the dream. They're the most farmed of all, they believe the dream is real life, with real meaning. That's what they're searching for.

One had a touch of Yusmely in her looks. For a cup of coffee, a megaburger, and some pleasantness, she provided the information for Yusmely's US passport. She even went away to get some shots taken and have them authenticated by on-mall security. Just for a souvenir of a very pleasant young American lady. And twenty dollars, cab fare, safely home. But she wanted to sit and chat; told me her entire life's story, and it took me a long time before I figured out she thought she'd gotten lucky. The realisation made me feel uneasy; I wasn't looking for sex on the hoof, not from the pre-starved.

There was so much I couldn't do because Ilana wasn't with me, and so much aimless time on my hands. I was bored.

I wished the drop-out well, salved my conscience with another twenty dollar bill, blinked, and went back to my hotel.

Television wasn't much, the Gideon wasn't much, so I ordered a bottle of Scotch and commenced getting myself utterly drunk, sitting on the verandah, watching the stars.

Just to see if it worked I got the drop-out's photo and began to grind off the photo with an electric razor. It took a long while, but that was all right. It still wasn't even midnight. Then I got Yusmely's photo from my bag and pasted it onto the photo and weighed the lot down with the hotel's Gideon.

Thankfully, I got drunk easily and quickly, and when I woke up another day had gone. The chores for that day I could have done in my sleep and I spent the day wishing I was asleep. The days, the chores, the lies, came and went, slowly.

It was a savage, a purely savage, unsanctified, savage bliss, when the aircraft touched down and I was home, again, in Brazil. Half an hour away from Ilana.

I arrived unannounced. It was the wrong time of the day, after siesta and before dinner. We were all a little embarrassed at the sudden reunion. I had been away a month; they'd become used to my absence, established their own routine. I'd become estranged to their natural ways. All was too abruptly unsettled, a hiatus catching at each gesture, between each outburst of words. And then a vacant silence we all tried to fill at once, and missed.

Ilana hugged and kissed me, and insisted that we go upstairs to our room. She took me rapidly by the hand and led me, tugging me behind her, and giggling, slightly. But there was something wrong. It wasn't as if she'd become loving and caring and anxious the moment she'd seen me again, as I had with her. I needed to be in silence with her. Silence between us, silence around us. And darkness, pitch black darkness where we could find our way to each other again.

Something banal and evil had happened. I understood for the first time that expression. I experienced it. Something banal and evil had crept silently into our relationship. Something banal had caused a change, in me, in her, in us.

She made of herself a joyous celebration for me. It was an act of duty, was too much too quick too excited too relentless. This feast of sexuality was not the communion I needed or longed for to break the loneliness of my absence. I should never, never, have left her.

There was a quiet desperation deep within me, and I tried to banish it. I made many unbidden promises. In the heat of the room and the turmoil of the bed, the alien strangeness and shadow, the self-conscious nakedness and the minor lack of fluency in the way we were now having · sex with each other, in the enthusiasm with which we were trying to fool each other, I tried to talk with her, to find her, again, my Ilana. But she was most boisterously there, joyous and loving and considerate, anticipating and pre-obedient to my every whim, and most utterly mine. And not there, not at all, as if she were impersonating the woman she used to be.

I lay aside and she asked me what was wrong. And I didn't know.

I had lost her. I didn't know it then.

'I'm sorry,' she said. 'Things will get better. Please believe me.'

So she felt it too, this banal presence, or banal absence.

And she tried in many ways to annealed me of my despair, my aimlessness and frettings and my impatient and exasperation with the darkness and formalised, academically structured madness of the species we belonged to.

I didn't know what I was trying to say.

How can a species be its own greatest, most dangerous predator, how can it organise its affairs with such incompetence in comparison to other species? How can a man be his own worst enemy? How can a man create his own evil, his own doom?

She hushed these thoughts away with kisses and her body and her beauty. In an abstracted, detached state, my eyes glaring at the act from a great distance, I took her. And blessedly, after the long, harsh climax, I fell into sleep, for a brief, mad bout of sleep. When I awoke she was lying peacefully in my arms, her eyes wide and questioning. On her forearms, at her shoulders, there were large, ugly red marks, welts, where someone had grabbed her very violently and shook her, relentlessly. Where I had, oh Jesus.

'It's not a problem,' she whispered, and moved her face closer to mine, 'It's not a problem. You know I know that's true. It's not a problem for me.'

Life between two people should be a story well told in the telling. What had happened to us, where were the interwoven stories well told that once were us?

We showered in almost total silence with each other, each of us afraid to smile. For fear the smile might break open, and some unseeable, intangible poison materialise into its presence and our doom, the end of our story, before our very eyes.

When I opened the room-door I nearly fell over Papa, standing there innocently, expectantly, and worried. She hushed him down the stairs ahead of her and he ran frightened and delighted, his tail wagging with puppyish happiness.

Maria and Yara were long fast now in their new relationship, mother and mature daughter, but Maria had the role of daughter, and was wastedly old and happy in it, trying in her second childhood to keep up with all the innovations Yara so lightly and constantly introduced. They paid a happy but formalised attention to me, and were fluently at ease only with Ilana.

Between themselves, in their own happiness and contentment, and conversation of things whose reference or relevance I didn't know, they domestically, in a solid, family manner, set the table for dinner, and set out the food. And the wine; for me. They were all smiling at that, to entice me into their ambit. If it had been a physical place I would have gone there, immediately, whatever the cost in any way. I just couldn't get into it. The more I tried the more out-of-place and excluded I felt.

'Remember the first night you came here?' Ilana asked, 'And we went to the Central Bar. And I bought that bottle of cheap whiskey. You were so happy then. You should have seen your eyes. They were so beautiful.'

It sounded so fucking patronising, as if she were coaxing a child to create from other memories a happy past that had never existed.

'I can't stand this. I'm sorry. I need air. I need to get into the air. I'm sorry.'

They were upset. They bustled and pleaded and it was genuine. They didn't want this to happen. That made it more pressing for me to get out. And finally, reluctant and abashed and letting me see how innocently guilty they looked, they let me go. Outside in the air I wanted to put my head against something cool and hard and rest my mind. But I couldn't even bring myself to stop at my favourite bench.

In the Central Bar I ordered two large whiskies. Yes. Very funny. Now just bring me the fucking things. So they brought me the two double whiskies in separate glasses and left me alone. All it does is ease the breathing, that's all. And I felt I hadn't had a breath in four hours. At least now I could feign a smile when I ordered more whiskey. Then I had a lonely, companionable cigarette and breathed yet again more deeply.

I had to salvage this situation. I had to salvage it. Life would not bring this gift again. I had to save it. I couldn't let all the beauty that was to me all of Ilana escape from my life. I had to search and find her again; and didn't she understand that? I had to find out where she'd gone.

Yusmely, looking anxious for the first time in her life, was standing at the other side of the table, obediently waiting for me to notice her. I smiled, naturally and without thought of it, for a moment.

'Yusmely!'

'Sylvia's been missing for more than a month,' she said.

'Sylvia?'

'Do you know anything about this?'

'No.'

'She always said she was afraid of you.'

'She's a stupid old woman,' I said. 'Sit down.'

But she didn't obey.

'Please, Yusmely. I've something important to tell you.'

'Yara said she'd break my neck if I ever came near to you again.'

Oh God. What worried them? This child?

'Please, Yusmely.' But she continued to stand.

'I have a US passport for you. A genuine US passport.'

'Oh God,' she said, with no breath, as if she had just inherited paradise. 'Oh God. Are you telling me the truth? Is this true?'

The excitement and happiness on her face was beautiful. This is what I'm probably best at, I thought, rescuing stray cats and frightened mice. At least they can be saved, and I know in my soul I can not. I sold it all to shovel snow. I sold what could be saved in me to shovel fucking snow, on the campus of a university innocent of the promises made in its name. Sold what I could have saved in myself to sell my own blood.

Ilana hadn't changed. From any back door she may have begged at, she hadn't watched her dreams being stolen, and then denied, hadn't found that the gain was the privilege of selling her own blood, literally.

Yusmely sat down, staring at me. No immigrant swearing the Oath of Allegiance ever had as much love and fealty in her entire body as Yusmely had in every fibre of her body. I waited until she had a cup of coffee, and was somewhat composed, before I coached her on passing, unnoticed, through the airport. Chew gum, lots of gum, and sneer at everyone like you own the place but don't particularly like it. And treat all officials like they're creeps, real slimy creeps just wanting a chance to get you spread on your back with your panties off and your legs wide open. And you sure know it too. They're yuks. That expression. Keep it on your face.

I told her where she'd been born, the name of the school she went to, the names of some of the teachers there, her mother's maiden name, where her Mom and Pop had been born. Her lips moved as she anxiously repeated the information to herself and passed it on into hard, solid, rote memory.

But the passport, where was the passport?

I said I'd have two more whiskies, and buy a bottle, have them put it in a bag. Then we'd go back to the Napoli. I'd go upstairs, put my bottle safely to bed, put her passport in the bag, and drop it down to her. OK?

OK.

There were volumes of silent, polite queries in her eyes.

When I knocked on the door of the Napoli, Papa barked. Maria opened the door. She smiled at me. Yara too, and she asked me how I was. Ilana was straight-faced, just a glimmer of anger, and a dark stain of tears under her eyes. She ignored me.

I said I was going to bed and went upstairs. I put a few twenty dollar bills in with the passport, for safety scribbled the pertinent information again on the bag, opened the jalousies, and tossed the bag down to Yusmely. She took out the passport, stared at it, checked it everyway, and kissed it. From two flights up I could see the love and adoration in her eyes. She blew me a kiss, afraid to make a noise, mouthing Thank You.

Then she turned and ran away up the street, just like the child she still was. Just like a condemned prisoner pardoned on the eve of execution, given freedom, and the chance of happiness.

I closed the jalousies, took off my shoes and socks, got a towel, wrapped it about my neck, and squatted down against the wall with my bottle of whiskey.

Ilana had a bottle of wine in her hand when she opened the door, and Papa looked affronted when she turned again to close the door in his face.

'Let the beast in.'

'He used to sleep there,' she said. 'Where you're sitting, when you were away.'

'I'm never going away again.'

She opened the door and he came in and looked at us, as if he wanted to broker peace between us. You'll be twice affronted, Papa, when they don't admit you to the kingdom of paradise. Or don't you have such mad dreams, like a human? After some consideration of me he settled under the bed. When she went to sit on the bed she misjudged it slightly and plopped down heavily onto it. Papa startled and scampered out again, and went back to squat at the door, meekly refusing to take offence at the rudeness of his mistress. This wasn't her first bottle of wine. It was O'Higgins Vineyard wine, from Chile.

'I'm sorry, Ilana.'

'What were you doing with Yusmely, please?'

'How did you know that?'

'What were you doing with Yusmely, please?'

As if I don't have a name, Ilana, the name you gave me.

'Fuck you.'

She didn't know this hurt so much. She does not intend this pain. She could not intend this pain. I knew that.

Ilana, I love you. Only you. I love you, Ilana. You know that. You know that's true, Ilana.

'I brought Yusmely a present. A US passport. She was afraid of Yara so I threw it down to her.'

'I know.'

'How?'

'Papa would never bark at you. He loves you. He used to sleep there, where you're sitting, when you were away.'

'I know. You told me.'

'Yes. I forgot. You know everything. Excuse me.'

'I'm also lovelier than you are, and my legs are more beautiful. My breasts are more beautiful. And my lovely bum can pout more beautifully than Madam's.'

Her head snapped up and she looked at me, as inquisitively and curiously as Papa. Just a pinch of a smile was playing about her face.

'You're such a poor, lost little girl, all alone in the world,' she said, and used my name.

'Just because you went to private schools, and learned to forgive more than I can. I never had your opportunities, Ilana, to learn to forgive. You forget that, I never had your opportunities.'

'I can tell mad stories of a multilingual mouse in Kerry who always has a fur coat and white gloves, and a big timid elephant in Africa who dreams of being a sleek cat in Amsterdam.'

'I can make bigger, badder mistakes than you can; and I'm very, very sorry, Ilana. I apologise.'

She bowed her head and began to smile.

'It's all right,' she said, 'I understand you.'

'That's just because you read Gideon in megastar hotels, and teach the composition of creative literature to the huddled middle-classes yearning to be racing drivers.'

She began to laugh, and wiped away a tear.

'And Judas saith unto Jesus: 'And just why didst thou set me up, Skinflint? What's thirty grand to you, for God's sake? Now I'll be crucified forever.' So they executed Judas, and the world lived happily everafter. Just like a nice, proper story; for weeping young ladies with emotions as sensitive as gunpowder.'

'*Stop!*' She took a relieved, long sip from the bottle, placed it on the night table, and started to undress herself.

'I had a right to be angry with you,' she said.

'Yes.'

She settled herself into the bed, and shook out her hair.

'I still want to be angry with you,' she said, and patted the side of the bed. 'Come and sit here. Let Papa go to sleep.'

The welts on her upper arms and shoulders were red and sore looking.

'Were you awake when I did that?'

'I think so, in a way. I thought you were going to split me apart. That's not a joke. It's better if you put your arms about my bottom when you're in that mood.'

'OK.'

'I know how you felt this afternoon. I was too frantic. I couldn't pause. You left that rich country and all the credit card girls, to come back to me. In my heart I had never believed it. When I saw you again I felt like a tarantula looking at her mate. I couldn't stop salivating. Now I know how you felt, then. I forgive you.'

'Ilana, in one restaurant, a gold card restaurant, — where else dare I ask, — I asked the waitress to put a little snip of lemon rind in my coffee. The manager came and asked me just what my problem was.'

An hour later we were still awake, talking about everything, the price of bread and the fate of the world. Just talking to each other. Happy as cats licking milk.

She dozed a little, still sitting up in bed, her eyes closed for a few moments and her breathing went deeper.

Her head shook something away, and as her eyes were trying to blink open she asked: 'What happened to Sylvia?'

'Sylvia?'

'Maria said you had her killed.'

'Maria's gone strange, Ilana.'

'Yes. She's failing. When we go to church each morning she thinks the priest is the Messiah. Every morning Yara has to stop her walking on her knees up to the altar.'

'Is that where you go each morning?'

'It was the first morning, the day after you brought Yara back. She was grateful. We were both grateful. I told Yara it was serious and she must be grateful to you. She knew it already. When she told Maria the next day that she'd been to confession and holy communion, Maria didn't believe her and went to the priest to ask. It was the shock turned her senile. She knows where Yara comes from, where we both come from. Now she adores Yara. Every morning they go to confession, mass, and holy communion together. And Yara is afraid to tell the priest.'

'Tell him what?'

'What? Don't you know?'

'What, Ilana?'

'Maria is Jewish. That is what her postal husband wanted. A Jewish bride. But she's forgotten almost everything now about her life, except that she was married to a schmuck.'

'Do you go to church also, Ilana?' A big grinning smile spread across her face. 'Only to mass, to keep them company.' But she kept deliberately smiling that knowing grin at my worrying anticipation.

'I won't tell any priest that you're just a normal male,' she said. 'And that you're in the prime of your strength. A man of serious character, and always in the prime of his strength. I won't tell anyone, I promise.'

She turned away smiling to herself and slid down in the bed.

She was sleepy, now, a child's sleepiness, and she wanted to push it away, wanted to taste and cherish more of her happiness, to keep it deeply alive for future memory.

I would do anything, I would do amazing things, to keep her safe and secure. She knew that, watching me, with still that aura of female vulnerability eternally about her.

'Come into bed. I want to smell your skin, I want to feel your skin. Be soft and warm and kind to me tonight.'

'Yes.'

'When you ran away today.'

'I didn't run away.'

'You did. You walked out. You left me without you.'

Ilana, I drank four large whiskies in the Central Bar. I didn't know why I had walked out on you. Pressure in my mind, claustrophobia in my mind. I saw Yusmely; Yusmely robbed and cheated and denied and stripped of everything except her very life and her youth, and turned into a whore, not just a sexual whore, and looking everywhere, everyway, for one half chance to rob a little bit of it back. I saw you and Yara and Yusmely and Solange and me and a thousand more I have known; robbed most cheap of what we hold most dear. In the dining room with you and Maria and Yara I felt out of place, felt unworthy to be among you, felt less than you, felt so uneasy, so sensitive among you, as if I carried a wound. My mind will not let me forget, my mind will not forgive me. I was trying to run away from that. I saw the nervous anguish in Yusmely's eyes and I learned that, then. I came back to you, to ask you to forgive me, only to hear you say it, and then to leave; I did not expect forgiveness, only its words. Because we got the fuckers back, Ilana, you and me. We suckered them back. And still my mind will not let me forget: I was suckered cheap for what I once held most dear, all the dreams of my life. All the dreams of my life held then.

'I forgive you,' she said. 'I have never said that before in my life. I forgive you, only you. And you must value that. You must value that now or you must leave me now.'

'I know how to value it, Ilana. I don't know how to accept it. I wasn't cultured to accept forgiveness. You wouldn't forgive me if you knew what I am inside.'

'I know you are damaged. I know that. I saw it the first time I saw you. I have seen many damaged men from Europe arrive on the docks, seamen and illegal immigrants. Once I asked Yara if Europeans thought our country was a sanatorium for all their defeated people. She said "Why not? There's no other place left for them to go. They're like us." We understand how it feels to be robbed of our dreams, to be left with the emptiness of stolen dreams. I knew it when I saw you. You were not foreign or strange to me. I saw your eyes when you first saw me. I loved you then. I love you now.'

My hand was on her shoulder, squeezing it, kneading it, squeezing it hard, very hard. And she paid it no attention.

'It's difficult for me to hate my father,' she said. 'He deserves my hate. And I hate him. I hate even his memory. I was healthy and loving and he deserted me. I can see him in my mind. I spit on him. I spit on Mama. I spit on their memory.

I want you to do the same, now. You must do the same. You must do the same. Spit on them. Spit on those who damaged you. Spit on them, spit on their graves, spit on their children, spit on their memory. Write it down. That they are the revolting, sick essence of the vomit of spit. That is their character, that is their only characteristic: *the vomit of spit.*'

'Tenha calma, Ilana, tenha calma.'

But it was gone. The damage was healed, finally healed. The days, the years, of cigarettes and sedatives and alcohol

were gone. All the pain, to which my drugs were palli-
atives, was gone.

I didn't know what to say, and after a moment I said: 'Do
you want babies, Ilana?'

And she twisted under my hands, laughing out loud and
twisted back to me and said: 'Oh yes please. Buy me some.
As many as you like. Get them on a gold card at La Galleria,
— "Does Sir require the items deluxed for carrying or shall
I limousine them to your hotel, Sir?" —' And twisted away
again, unable to control her laughter.

'It was a serious question,' I said.

'I know that,' she said, still laughing. 'Yara hasn't had a
man in seven months and goes to church every day and
she's still taking her tablet every day. And me too.'

She was snug beside me and after a few minutes I
thought she'd gone to sleep. I put my hand down onto her
stomach because she liked that when she was sleeping and
it somewhat lessened the intensity of her nightmares. She
made a little noise and placed my hand as she wanted it on
her stomach, exactly as she wanted it on her stomach. When
she got it right she made another sound of approval. It
wasn't necessary for me to fully wake up for her
nightmares. Half asleep I could hold her and soothe her. I
never expected these nightmares to stop, and when she
began to move, and to turn towards me I thought it was
beginning. She asked me if I were awake, really awake.
Because she wanted to tell me, of the house in Recife, and
the bedlam of the nightmares of the children every night.
And how a woman there made promises to her, and kept
those most sacred, childish promises, and told her there
was a girl exactly from the same situation and now she was
very happy where she was. And she agreed to go to that
place too.

There she met Yara, twelve years old and boisterous and

quick and difficult and always bold and loved like a little sister by even the hardest nuns. All those years, so close to Yara, who loved her and fought for her and fought with her. Two little girls each giving the other a childhood. Until Yara suddenly and directly said she couldn't stand it any more, she was too randy for men, she had to get out and have one. Big and strong and stinking, reeking, of maleness, and young male hunger, and full of courtships and deceits and stratagems. But she would love him anyway, and he would really love her too. Because she was a woman, and possessed these miraculous powers of transformation.

They talked of nothing else for months. And her sexual instincts jumped alive in her body like a punch from nature. Yara stole some old books; she said she was not proud of this and she was speaking truthfully, believe me.

They walked out unnoticed at midday, just after Yara stole a handful of brass candlesticks. No, not in Recife, in Santa Catarina. At nightfall they couldn't even remember that they had ever had sexual passions. They were too terrified, and took the last bus from the station. Because it was the last bus; and they daren't stay out on the streets at night. The bus only stopped to change drivers, get more petrol, for three days and nights.

Without eating, drinking only water. Then Yara made them take the next bus in the next station and it went on for three days and three nights. They had to sell the books and the candlesticks to people who bought them out of charity. Chocolate bars and water for three days. They knew nothing when they arrived here. Very sore bottoms and very groggy, as if they had arrived, totally unrested, from the moon. They came to the Napoli because Yara couldn't remember her father and always imagined him as an Italian. Even then she took to Maria like a daughter, as if they were kin. But Yara was hungry for money, now.

Wanted money more than she wanted a man. She saw men
now in a different way. So she went direct to Sylvia.

'This is all I have to tell you,' she said. 'Any sailor I took I
took because they were lovely boys and I liked them and I
would have slept with them anyway. When they gave me
money afterwards I took it. Many times I just brought them
to the Central Bar and asked them for money because I had
saved them the taxi fare. If I didn't like them I didn't go
with them. That's why Sylvia made my life so hard.

'I was ashamed to come back to Maria. Until I met you.
She knew I would not come back with a man unless I was
bringing my husband home. I saw Maria many times in the
streets and her eyes always told me to come back. I
couldn't. Even sitting at the docks there was some hope,
some life. To be a defeated little daughter at home with
Maria was an unbearable, despairing thought in my mind.
Maria knew that, too.

'Maria knows nothing of tablets, she cannot understand
them. When I came back with my belongings from Sylvia's
she told me not to make you use the plastic bag, that's what
she calls condoms, in Italian, the little plastic bag. She said
not to use it; that you needed a baby, hmm? That a baby
would make you recover. I thought she meant one of those
warm, smelly, soft dependent things that Yara becomes
erotic about, they're so kissable and huggable with all the
love and forgiveness they give and give and give. But that
wasn't the kind of baby you wanted. Maria was wrong. Just
once.'

She cuddled to me, wiped and sniffed away her tears,
and went to sleep. That night her nightmare was slight,
very slight, no more than an irksome dream. When it was
finished she pulled me about the bed to suit herself, put her
left arm under my head and her right hand on my back and
pulled me fast to her, make herself comfortable, and made a

sound of approval. In the morning she awoke bright and sparkling and bit me on the shoulders with her lips: 'Bom dia, mi amo.'

Here, the story closes. In no way, not even fictionally, can my mind give up this woman.

In my nightmare, each time I sleep, I see a passenger train, empty, pulling away from the station, from there to here. And I see the red light in my mind.

FICTION *from* WOLFHOUND PRESS

DRINKER AT THE SPRING OF KARDAKI

Linda McNamara

'These tales . . . have a rich, sure-footed prose that makes Linda McNamara a name to watch out for.' *(U Magazine)*

THE ATHEIST

Seán Mac Mathúna

'Stylish, subversive, satirical and sexy short stories.' *(Dublin Opinion)*

IRISH POETRY NOW: OTHER VOICES

Ed Gabriel Fitzmaurice

The latest and best of Irish poetry from some sixty poets publishing in the 1980s and 1990s. A variety of voices and range of subjects that celebrates the breadth and confidence of the new and emerging poets.

WHERE THE TREES WEEP

Dolores Walshe

A new writer of power and imagination.

'There is a sureness both of technique and content that shows the hand and mind of a true writer.' *(Sunday Press)*

THE TWO WOMEN OF AGANATZ

Frank Golden

Shunned by travellers, the sole inhabitants of Aganatz are Olan and her daughter Liano and even they have not dared to explore all its winding corridors and abandoned rooms. Hadge, a traveller lost in the desert is rescued from death. And the story begins.

ANCESTRAL VOICES

Hugh FitzGerald Ryan

The haunting story of Jack Dempsey whose relationship with his Wexford-born bride Elaine is enmeshed in his need to investigate the infamous tragedies of the peasant revolt of 1798.

Write for our complete catalogue
WOLFHOUND PRESS
68 Mountjoy Square, Dublin 1, Ireland